Keene looked up and saw her.

"Still think I'm an old lush?" she asked, standing there naked, running her hands over her smooth body. It was the body of a woman no longer young, but female—female and somehow very pale and too soft. "Old lush, huh? Ever see a body like this on an old lush?" Her hands ran down her flesh and up again.

He stood staring at her, almost transfixed, and watched her stretch her naked woman's body on the wrinkled sheets. He watched her trying to force some semblance of remembered coyness into the features of her face and heard her say in the bygone voice of another time's seduction, "Take me. You can have what you want."

Sick, nauseated, Wally Keene picked up his coat and, without looking at her, walked out of the apartment.

5:45 to Suburbia

Vin Packer

PROLOGUE BOOKS

F + W Media, Inc.

Published in electronic format by
PROLOGUE BOOKS
an imprint of F+W Media, Inc.
10151 Carver Road
Blue Ash, Ohio 45242
www.prologuebooks.com

eISBN 10: 1-4405-3717-8
eISBN 13: 978-1-4405-3718-2
POD ISBN 10: 1-4405-5808-6
POD ISBN 13: 978-1-4405-5808-5

This is a work of fiction. Names, characters, corporations, institutions, organizations,
events, or locales in this novel are either the product of the author's imagination or,
if real, used fictitiously. The resemblance of any character to actual persons (living or
dead) is entirely coincidental.

This work has been previously published in print format as a Gold Medal Book by
Fawcett Publications, Inc., New York, NY.

5:45 TO SUBURBIA

CHAPTER ONE

"Ever hear of a C-cup bitch before?" Wally Keene had asked Charlie once.

"She's the worst kind of bitch there is, Charlie! She's as power-happy as she is top-heavy. Our business is brimming over with them—ours and advertising. Her bosom bosses her body and she bosses you. . . . Hell, *you* know the type, Charlie. Tell her a joke and she heard it last February; but she knows 'a new one' you haven't heard. Take her to lunch and she sends back the Gibson, because the onion isn't crisp. In a conference room when you try to win a point by throwing in a random statistic to make it more effective, she's the one who sends out for the *World Almanac,* and finds out there were nowhere near 7,140 automobiles stolen in Houston in 1955. . . . Just imagine Scarlett O'Hara playing Kitty Foyle, and you got a C-cup bitch. Better still, Charlie, take a look around you . . . at Marge Mann, for instance."

Charlie had seen her in the back of the elevator as he had come in that morning; and for some reason as he stood pressed against the other passengers and rode in gloomy 8:55 A.M. silence to 16, he was reminded of Wally's description of her. Reminded of how he had hated young Keene for saying it (Keene had made the remark about a year ago in the bar at the Commodore, where they were both waiting for the 6:30 to Greenwich); and how he had hated him for being so amusingly accurate about Marge. About her type; about his own effortless admission to himself that she *was* a type; so what,

7

Charlie had thought, who isn't. . . . Still, it had made him
angry; and he realized rather uncomfortably, it had
made him feel some vague sense of guilt too.

He had seen her standing back there with the feather
in her hat; smiled at her, and wished he had winked instead; and after he had thought of Wally's year-old
remark, he had recalled one of his own, years and years
older; one of his own to Marge: "Wear a hat with a
feather on it, and meet me at the Fiftieth Street Entrance to Saks."

It sounded oddly prosaic to Charlie's memory; sounded
more like two old ladies off on a shopping spree than
lovers bent on a clandestine rendezvous; but even so,
Charlie knew he still couldn't pass Saks without flinch-
ing; couldn't look at one of Marge's hats without telling himself, too often and too insistently, that he had
really been in love wih her; my God, he had even considered divorcing Joan. *Seriously* considered it; hadn't
he?

When the elevator came to a stop he did an awkward
thing that turned out to be pointless. Before he got
out he looked back at Marge, wanting perhaps to improve on his initial greeting, wanting to add more to it,
to make it less incidental; and instead, as he looked
around, the man behind Charlie moved forward abruptly, so that both bumped noses; and the collision resulted
in clumsy apologies, muttered as the two men stepped
quickly out of the elevator, and in Charlie's not having
a second glance at Marge. He was sorry about that, particularly sorry about it because of the past month's ten-
sion around Cadence Publications; and because somehow he wanted to reassure Marge that he was pulling
for her. Pulling for her against Wally Keene.

Wally had said something else to Charlie about Marge
once, not very long ago. A week or two ago. Wally had
said, "Charlie, you want to hear something funny? This
will break you up! The other night that bitch *offered*
herself to me. That's right, she offered herself to me!
That wizened old bitch stretched herself out on a hide-

a-bed like a slab of white lamb sacrificed on an altar! And you know what she said, Charlie, you know what she had the nerve to say? She said, 'All right, you can have what you want. All right, take me!' " Wally had held his sides laughing. "I mean, God, can you picture it!"

Charlie didn't believe it; didn't believe for a minute Marge Mann would do anything like that—not for any-one, not even for her job. She used to tell Charlie, back when they were close, "The reason I like you, Charles, is that I like myself when I'm with you. I think that's important." That was like her; that was the way she was. . . . So Charlie didn't believe Keene's story.

Pushing through the wide glass doors, Charlie entered the reception room of Cadence Publications.

He looked right for these surroundings; at home in them. For a middle-aged man who lived well and was unlikely ever to become calorie-conscious (just on prin-ciple) Charlie Gibson had a good strong body that was tall and broad; and could still carry a single-breasted suit well enough to make many of his chunky colleagues envious.

He dressed that body well too. He had a feel for style and taste in his wardrobe; and a manner in his bearing, his stance and his gait, that announced he was right. *Distingúe*, some would have said of this man in the dark blue suit, with the thick crop of coal-colored hair streaked thinly with gray. Seeing him on this morning, some would have insisted *handsome* as well. For when Charlie's round face was sullen in thought, with the wide deep brown eyes somber, he seemed almost hand-some; seemed, ironically, younger too, and not as aver-age of countenance. Nor as shy and vulnerable as he did when he had nothing bothering him.

As he strode across the thick gray carpet, passing the plush red leather couches and round white oak tables, one of the Cadence magazine covers stared up at him from a table top. It was their mystery magazine, *The Suspects,* one of the twenty magazines Cadence published. A picture of a semi-nude blonde with blood running from her mouth, rushing down a rickety staircase, adorned its front. Charlie winced, made a mental note to get a memo off to the editor, and thought, as he mumbled a "morning" to the receptionist, of what Bruce Cadence had said yesterday.

"Look, Charlie, I don't like it either. We've always had a good name in our field—always—except for that incident with our comic line. But that incident cost us plenty, Charlie. Now we've got to recover."

Charlie had argued, "But we won't recover making the same mistake we made with the comics. Sexy covers, lurid blurbs. Is this how we're going to recover? . . . And a brand new exposé magazine we're ashamed to put the Cadence name on!"

"The heat was on comics, Charlie. That's all."

"And it won't be turned on our other books?"

"No, Charlie, it won't be. Providing we stay in bounds, of course. It's different with a children's audience, you know that. They're always worrying about what Johnny *should* read, when they're not worrying about if Johnny *can* read."

"Still and all, Bruce, Cadence doesn't have to cheapen the line to sell!"

"Not *cheapen* the line, Charlie. You know I don't mean that. Just make it less staid, as Keene says."

"By exposing people?"

"Charlie, I know you're opposed to the new magazine. I *know!* But do you have a better suggestion? . . . We're in a hole, Charlie. We're in a canyon!"

Before Charlie had left Cadence's office, Bruce Cadence had added: "You'll get the dummy tomorrow. After you make any corrections, rush it up to me. Okay, Charlie?"

It wasn't okay. A lot of other people at Cadence felt the way Charlie did. No one—not even Charlie—had gone on record as being fighting-mad-vehemently-opposed to the new magazine; but even as it went around in dummy form, the nickname for it which someone had thought up, stuck. . . . Unofficially, it was called *Vile*.

Vile was Wally Keene's brainchild. Bruce Cadence had hired young Keene as a troubleshooter, telling Charlie that he was convinced that the organization needed "new blood. Fresh blood, Charlie, *young* blood!"

Vile was the fruit of the new, fresh, young blood.

Down at the end of the long corridor on the 16th floor was the pine-paneled office of the Executive Editorial Director at Cadence. This was Charlie's office, and the panoramic view of West Manhattan midtown to the Hudson, from its windows, was one Charlie never tired of seeing as he walked in there every morning; a scene he never failed to appreciate—the same way he was aware of and warm toward the fragrance of his secretary's perfume at the beginning of a work day. Bonnie sat just outside his door and she always wore Arpege. She always looked up just as he passed the row of telephones on her desk; always smiled; always said, "Good morning, Mr. Gibson. I'll be right with you," and always appeared five minutes from the time she said that.

So ten minutes after Charlie had hung up his coat, without having yet seen her, he began to suspect that something was wrong; that perhaps she was sick (she never *was*); or that perhaps there was some new intrigue transpiring, a situation that invariably seemed to decimate the normal routine in the office, because usually the secretaries were the first to know, and the last to savor the enjoyment. Haphazardly he glanced through the pile of mail on his desk, at the same time pressing the buzzer which would call Bonnie, if she were near enough to be called. As he was doing this, some slight resentment starting to rise in him, as it always did when his meticulous sense of organization seemed threatened, a newspaper clipping fell from an envelope he held in his hand.

It was clipped from the *Times;* a brief write-up of the dinner a charitable organization had given in Charlie's

honor several weeks ago, in appreciation of his capabili-
ties as a fund-raiser. Above the write-up, there was a
rather poor photograph of Charlie, a shoulders-up, smiling shot. Across his face was scribbled something Charlie
did not have time to read before he heard the sound of
the singing.

He looked up, puzzled at Bonnie; puzzled and then
bemused. He had forgotten all about it.

"Happy Birthday," she said, holding the tiny cake out
to him; grinning; a slim, baby-faced girl, not too much
older than Charlie's daughter, but less spoiled than Jane
—and wiser, Charlie had a hunch; quicker. "And many
happy returns, Mr. Gibson."

She set it on his desk; a candle sagged in the icing,
dripping and flickering.

"Forget?" she asked him.

"I sure did."

"Well, make a wish and blow it out."

It was uncanny that at the same time she said that to
him, Charlie's eyes fell for a slow second to the sealed
interoffice memo that was lying beside his mail pile;
and that he thought as he looked at it: I wish that
weren't on my desk; wish I didn't have to read that;
uncanny, because Charlie had no real idea what the
memo contained.

"Did you make a wish?"

"Yes," Charlie said, deciding good health was a sound
one, then blowing the candle out. "There!"

"I won't ask how old you are."

"Fifty."

"You didn't *have* to tell, Mr. Gibson. I wasn't fishing."

"I suppose that sounds old, hmm, Bonnie? To you?"

Charlie glanced up at her. She said, "Yes, frankly . . .
Want a piece with some coffee, or is it too early?"

"Much too early. Can we save it until after lunch?"

"Sure. Here, I'll take it." She leaned across for the
plate, and her eyes fell to the sealed memo. "I suppose
you saw *that*."

"Yes. Any idea what it's about?"

"I wouldn't like to speculate," she told him. She looked suddenly serious. "I just wouldn't like to."

"Did Keene's secretary leave it?"

"Uh-huh."

Charlie felt something sink inside of him; then again remembered the curl to Keene's lips that evening at the Commodore when he said, "Ever hear of a C-cup bitch before?"

As though she were reading his thoughts, Bonnie said, "You don't think Mr. Cadence *would* demote her, do you, Mr. Gibson?"

"You think that's what it's about, too?"

She nodded.

"I don't know, Bon," he answered. "I hope not."

"I think it would—kill her," the girl said. She lifted the cake plate from his desk, frowning. "I wish you'd open it now."

"After I've gone over *all* my mail, I will," Charlie said. "That's the only safe rule when it comes to these things. Open them last; that way the immediate business gets done before I blow my top."

"I know, Mr. Gibson." Bonnie sighed. "By now I know."

She started across the office toward the door. Charlie let himself enjoy her legs before he looked up and said, "Bon? By the way, you'll see that the dummy gets into me right away, won't you? I want it checked and upstairs by four."

"It's on your desk now," she answered. "Over on the left . . . And, Mr. Gibson, there's a letter from your daughter in the pile."

"Oh? Good!"

"Happy birthday again, Mr. Gibson." She smiled in the doorway. "You don't look fifty at all."

When she had gone, Charlie sat momentarily to wonder how he had managed to forget that it was the 6th of March; and then, vaguely pleased in imagining Jane had remembered it, he fumbled through the letters on his blotter to find hers, but stopped abruptly when he came across the newspaper clipping he had put aside. He picked up the envelope it had come in, saw no return address, and when he shook it saw no other clue as to its sender. Then he took the clipping and read the legend written there across his face.

It said simply: YOU SURE TURNED OUT TO BE AN UGLY S. O. B.—CLASS OF '28.

For the first time that morning, Charlie Gibson began to laugh.

MARCH 6, 1925

CHAPTER TWO

ON THE afternoon of Charles Gibson's 18th birthday, someone down the hall in the DKE house was playing *Second Hand Rose* on the phonograph; and Charlie was at his desk, bent over a composition for Poli. Sci., which began: "A year and three months ago today Lenin died at Gorki. It is appropriate to pause and remember—"

Whatever it was that was appropriate to pause and remember, Charlie had forgotten, for lately his mind was a jumble of tangled thoughts. He was a sensitive, serious sophomore who wanted to be a writer (a poet, preferably; except it didn't pay a goddam thing), and therefore a good 70% of his thoughts were centered on sex; a good 10% on sex with Mitzie Thompson (though Charlie switched the noun to 'love' in his mind where she was concerned); and the remaining percentage on what a bastard his old man was, what a crashing bore it was to be broke all the time, and what an effort it was to concentrate on anything "important" (meaning his writing) in a fraternity house at the University of Missouri.

Currently Charlie was under the influence of E. E. Cummings and Ezra Pound, when he was not under Mitzie's spell; and this afternoon he was coping with all three, as well as Lenin and *Second Hand Rose,* so that beside the composition, on a scrap of yellow second sheet, there was scribbled the beginnings of a poem entitled simply: *mitzie before breakfast.*

So far there was only one verse:

tell me how you like to see morning
come for us, say it sleepily
the way you said it then
we'll cuss awakening out of night
i love you when your arms hold me
so tight.

"What're you doing, Chazz boy?" a voice called from the doorway.

"Not too much." Charlie wouldn't have to look up to know it was Otto Avery speaking. He detested the way Avery persisted in calling him Chazz boy. But he did look up. He watched Avery saunter toward him, and thought, God, he's suave; he really is—no matter the rest, he really *is,* and said blandly: "What was the name of that revolutionary journal?" deftly pushing the yellow second sheet under his arm and out of sight. But Avery had noticed. Would he do anything?

"Which one?" Avery sat on the edge of the desk.

"The one Lenin edited. I'm writing a composition."

"*Iskra,*" Avery answered, filching the piece of yellow paper with a sudden jerk of his hand. "Meaning 'The Spark'." A grin came to his lips.

"Give it back," Charlie said.

"Mitzie before breakfast, eh?"

"Oh, come on now, damn it!" Charlie stood up and made a grab for his poem, but Avery was taller and quicker; he held it out of Charlie's reach.

"Chazz boy," he said, "is there something you ought to tell Uncle Otto?"

"Go to hell, for one thing."

"I'd had no idea the affair'd been consummated."

"Did you want something when you came in?"

"Really, Chazz boy, I think you should have at least confided in *me*. I'm quite hurt, Chazz. You know, I'm *offended*."

"Are you through with it?" By now his face felt hot, and he was sure it was very red; but his voice sounded only sullen, slightly bored.

"Mitzie rates some sort of punctuation, don't you think?" Avery chuckled. "A semicolon, or a dirty old comma, or something, Chazz boy?"

"I'm busy. Give it back and clear out."

Avery looked at him. Avery was uncommonly good-looking; he acted years older than he was—he was only nineteen, but he had polish. And very light blond hair with those keen blue eyes that penetrated their subject in a terrible, formidable gaze; and money, Avery had, and wit, and some certain power Charlie was forced to appreciate. Charm too.

"You really have it for Mitzie, don't you, Chazz?"

"Get out!"

"You really think she's the bee's knees, don't you, Chazz?"

"I'd like it back, Avery!" Charlie held his hand out.

"Oh, I'm going to give it back to you, Chazz. Chazz, you don't think I'm not going to return your poem to you, do you?"

"Well then, do it."

"Sure, Chazz, sure." Avery picked up a pencil from the desk, took a notebook from the back pocket of his knickers, and walked to the bed. "Sure, Chazz, boy. I'll give it back. . . . First I have to make a copy."

He sat on the bed and made the copy and Charlie sat frozen at his desk. Down the hall the phonograph record had been changed, and as Avery wrote, he sang along with it in some spots: "*Here's the Japanese Sandman, Sneaking on with the dew, Just an old secondhand man, He'll buy your old day from you.*"

Charlie was thinking: My God, I'm going to bawl. I feel like bawling!

But he broke his pencil in half instead, and sat there powerless to stop Avery. Worse, he didn't even try.

"Patience, Chazz boy," Avery murmured. "This won't take a minute . . . *Oh, here's the Japanese San-and-man—*"

Charlie Gibson met Otto Avery for the first time on the beginning day at the Kedd School for Boys. This was in 1919, and at twelve Charlie was somewhat shy; by no means unusually shy, but simply endowed with a normal amount of timidity which any boy would feel at his first break from home. Any boy but Otto Avery.

It was at midday during recreation in the playground on a sharp September morning that Charlie noticed Avery. Anyone would have noticed him before the other boys, just as in later life he was always the first to be recognized anywhere. He was exactly Charlie's height then, but more filled out than Charlie, sturdy and broad. Whereas Charlie was slightly sallow-complexioned, Avery was rosy and brown in color, and even then his blue eyes were alternately sparkling and piercing.

He was always laughing, calling out, on the move. He was a friendly, vivacious thirteen-year-old; but there was more in it than that. He used his breeziness to cover his secret designs. Even then, he was plotting how he could use everybody and everything to his advantage, and he was helped by the fact that he never had any morals whatever.

When Charlie noticed him for the first time he was standing in the middle of the yard telling a story to a group of other boys, and although he was as new to Kedd as Charlie was, he had already fascinated new and old boys, and they were laughing and joking with him as though he had been at Kedd for years.

Charlie stood off to the side watching the scene, unwilling as yet to walk up to the group—really, unable to—and envying Avery his self-assurance. Then, as though Avery had felt Charlie's presence behind him, and felt, telepathically, Charlie's unsureness, he had whirled around in the midst of a sentence and spotted Charlie and he had called out, "Hey there, boy, c'mon now. Join us!" and then added rather unnecessarily: "There's nothing to be afraid of!"

It was that final sentence of the greeting that Charlie resented, for he had never been "afraid." He had never felt patronage of this sort—and the sort to follow and in the face of it, instead of proving to Avery and everyone there in the courtyard that of course he was *not* afraid to join them at all, he simply wilted, wilted and went forth like a nervous misfit, tongue-tied and blushing.

That first day, in Charlie's mind, ruined every day to come. For from then on, Charlie never got the opportunity to redeem himself, to *be* himself. Avery more or less adopted him, and set about molding for Charlie a personality which was not Charlie's, but Avery's image of Charlie. From that moment on at Kedd, Avery patronized and mocked him.

It was at Kedd that Charlie was known by Avery's name for him—Chazz. "You know, Chazz," he used to tell Charlie years later, "I'll never forget how you looked that first morning at school—with your anxiety and politeness and helplessness. You were a mess, fellow, and where you'd have been if I hadn't looked out for you, I just don't know!"

Avery looked out for Charlie in a shaming kind of way. Avery was tremendously popular; and Charlie, rather negative and colorless in Avery's shadow. When another boy, in sport, twisted Charlie's arm, or kicked his behind, Avery would never let the sport grow to the inevitable point of comradeship, but would come up instead and insist, "Stop that! Chazz is under my protection. Didn't you know?"

And because Avery was strong and stoutly built, and everyone liked him, Charlie *was* let alone; the sport, which he had been enjoying as sport—even when he was not getting the better end—was terminated. And Charlie became, not disliked by the boys, but more—ignored, never ridiculed by them, save for Avery; but slighted

during horseplay, left to *observe* the nonsensical joking,
and punching and pillow-fighting that went on in the
dorms. Now and then, in a situation where the boys'
spirits were high and they were indulging in foolish
pranks among themselves, or wrestling one another on the
ground, Avery would approach Charlie and say, "I don't
know why I look out for you. You're such a goop. . . .
But it makes me feel better knowing you're under my
wing." He'd grin at Charlie and add, "Aren't you glad
of it?"

"No. I'm not."

"Oh, yes you are, Chazz boy, you're glad of it. Uncle
Otto knows."

There weren't many other thirteen-year-olds at Kedd
who knew as much about sex as Otto Avery did. He was
always holding a roomful of boys spellbound with lewd
stories about the things a man did to a woman. Like the
others, Charlie was fascinated too; and unlike many of
them, not particularly embarrassed. Leastwise, not at the
stories, nor at the elaborate descriptions in the stories; in
fact, Charlie was quite eager to hear. But Avery managed to spoil that for him too. In the middle of one, he
would glance across at Charlie and say: "Oh, but I *am*
sorry. Chazz boy, I didn't mean these words to fall on
your delicate ears. . . . I'm sorry, boys—but another time.
When Chazz isn't present."

"Don't be stupid!" Charlie would protest hotly. "What
do I care!"

"Oh, but *I* care," Avery would insist. "You're very sensitive. I know you are, and *you* know I know."

He would make it sound very cryptic and mysterious
before the others, as though Charlie had been confiding
in him; as though Charlie had told Avery once that that
sort of thing humiliated and embarrassed him.

When the boys would protest and shout for Charlie to
get out of the room then, if it bothered him so, Avery
would hold up his hand and announce: "Silence! I won't
have you making Chazz feel unwanted. He's as good as
you are—any of you—and better too."

It was a wonder to Charlie that anyone spoke to him
at all through those two years at Kedd. Later, when he
was fourteen and removed by his father to a public
school again, Charlie could only marvel at the curious
effect Avery had had on him; he could only sit and
wonder why he had never been able to push himself out
of that shell Avery had forced him into on the first day.
. . . But the only answer he ever came up with, was that
he had never experienced the emotion of hate before he
met Avery; he had never hated anyone or anything until
his encounter with Otto Avery, and he had not known
how to cope with it, not understood completely the
reasons for it; only wished the whole while that he had
never been sent to Kedd.

Out of it all, one incident stuck firmly in Charlie Gibson's mind. It was the same incident he thought of when
he first walked into the DKE house and saw Avery come
forward to greet him during fraternity rush week; and
it was the same incident he thought of that afternoon
while Avery sat on his bed copying the poem.

It happened during the second winter at Kedd. Charlie
was thirteen then, and resigned to his status at the
school, even resigned somewhat to Avery's unpleasant
attentions. Curiously enough, Charlie often found himself
wishing he were more like Avery and wishing, too, that
he could force Avery to submit to the same treatment
Avery forced on him. But on the afternoon in January
when the singular incident took place which Charlie
was never able quite to forget, or to understand completely, Charlie had no envy, nor any malice toward anyone.

He had just received his father's letter explaining that
a temporary setback in finances made it necessary to
withdraw Charlie from Kedd at the end of the term; and
he felt immensely jubilant; miraculously freed, like a
prisoner whose long sentence was suddenly, unexpectedly
rescinded. As he took his shower down in the locker
room after the three o'clock recreation hour, the warm
water rushing on his skin felt clean and good. And

Charlie felt much the same way, unburdened and nearly happy. He stayed under for an unusually long time, and it was just as he was planning to step out and turn off the faucets attached outside the stall, that the shocking stream of scalding water hit him. Frantically he pushed against the door in an effort to escape, but someone was holding him in.

"I say, Chazz boy, is it hot enough for you?"

"Let me out, Avery!"

"It doesn't *hurt*, does it? I wouldn't hurt you."

"Turn it off!" Charlie began to scream from the pain. "Avery, turn it off!"

"You won't get hot showers like this if you leave Kedd, Chazz boy."

"Avery, help me! Help!"

When Otto Avery finally did take his weight from the door, Charlie staggered out through the steam in tears; his flesh seared and stinging, while around him a small group of his classmates stood staring at him somewhat uncertainly. Perhaps a few wanted to sympathize with him, but none indicated it in Avery's presence. They simply stood woodenly, save for a few who snickered nervously as Charlie leaned naked against the brick wall of the room fighting for control.

Avery said simply, "We're all sorry we're losing you, Chazz boy. Things won't be the same." Then turning, waving, "Ta ta, Chazz."

Gradually the others went back to their own showering, leaving Charlie to collect himself; to stop his angry weeping; to dress and leave. Walking from the gym, he found Avery waiting for him.

"So you're going away," Avery said.

"I'm glad of it too."

"Oh, no you're not, Chazz. You mind it awfully. You mind it as much as you minded what happened just then." He put an arm on Charlie's shoulder. "It hurt, didn't it?"

"Of course it hurt!"

"It *really* hurt, didn't it?"

"Why don't you leave me alone?"

"I don't know, Chazz boy. It's always given me a kind of kick when you mind things. Why is that, do you suppose?"

"I don't know. Just get away!"

"I just wanted to show you I'll miss you next term, Chazz boy."

"You have a great way of doing it."

"It's *my* way, Chazzy. I get sort of a pleasure in seeing you wince. It's like—it's like—pulling your own hair to hurt yourself."

Then abruptly Avery stopped, removed his arm from Charlie's shoulder, hoiked and spat at the ground in a quick, defiant gesture. His eyes, when he looked back at Charlie, were dark and shining, the lucid color of them nearly blacked; and he said, "I could rub your face in that if I wanted to, Chazz."

"You're—crazy!" Charlie managed, staring at Avery.

"You should be like me," Avery said, "bold as brass and not giving a damn for anybody."

"Before I'd be like you I'd drown myself."

Avery laughed: "*I* almost drowned you, Chazzy, didn't I? Back there. Do you know I'm sorry for it . . . in a way . . . but only in a way, Chazzy."

He gave Charlie a mock salute and sauntered away from him.

It was the closest Charlie Gibson had ever come to seeing Otto Avery upset. And very vaguely Charlie understood that the reason was his leaving Kedd. Beyond that, he could only puzzle at Avery's mind; and oddly, for that slow second as he stood looking after Avery, feel sorry for him. And then, afraid. Of what? Charlie didn't know, but he had that sort of fear one feels when he looks back and realizes for the first time that at some point in his past he had been in great danger and never realized it.

Charlie never knew Avery was at the University until he saw him during the fraternity rush week. It was not at

all unlikely for him to be there; Avery's parents lived in
St. Louis; nonetheless, it shook Charlie up to see him
there. Charlie himself was the real interloper, for he was
from upstate New York, but against his father's violent
objections, he had come to Missouri to study at the
Journalism School. Avery surprised him a second time
by announcing he too was studying journalism.

"But I always thought you wanted to be an actor,"
Charlie said, after they had shaken hands in the DKE
living room and begun what Charlie felt would result
in an awkward conversation.

"Pater wouldn't hear of it." Avery smiled. "But there's
a fair drama department here, and I manage to work off
my thespian impulses. You look good, Chazz. You've
grown up."

"Yes, I have. And grown out of that name."

"Oh, you'll always be Chazz to me. . . . Remember
how I used to rag you at Kedd?"

"Quite clearly."

"I was an awful nincompoop, wasn't I? I hope I've
grown up too since then. . . . But say, you'll want to
meet the boys. Come along, Chazz. We have a fine
bunch here."

As he followed Avery, Charlie thought of that incident
at Kedd, thought: he *has* changed; I'd rather like him,
if he'd only stop addressing me as Chazz. And ultimately,
Charlie pledged Delta Kappa Epsilon, with Otto Avery
sponsoring him.

Of course, Avery hadn't changed at all; not really. He
had simply expanded; and there were several among
Charlie's pledge class whom Avery chose to "oversee."
He was less obvious than he had been with Charlie at
Kedd, but the effect was the same, if scattered. There
was always one boy he was riding, in that familiar joking
way of his, that pretended amiability, but invariably
managed through some sly strategy to show the boy up
as a fool; speciously dependent upon Avery for protection. He had a habit of inviting confidences, and then
exposing them before a host of people, tossing them in

much as one peppers a salad, as though there were
nothing unusual about his mentioning that this boy was
yet a virgin; ("I think it's a very noble quality," Avery
would announce, while the boy writhed in shame and
surprise at the suddenness of his exposure. "There're not
many of them left among males, except for lilies, of
course, and we all know he's no lily.") or that that boy
had a drastic fear of height ("I think it takes a brave man
to admit such a thing," Avery would say. "After all, most
people with silly fears like that are sissies, but we know
he's no sissy. He's just afraid of heights.").

During Hell Week, Avery took charge with an enthusiasm unmatched by any of the others. The three or
four scapegoats he had selected were the objects of the
most ludicrous and cruel tortures. One very shy freshman
was stripped of his clothes and left on a downtown
street corner, pushed out of a car, and made to run
frantically for some sort of shelter. And all the while
Avery insisted: "He's a great guy, but we've got to get
him over the complex he has. I only want to help him."
Adding, as was his way: "I'm going through more tor-
ture than he is, just thinking about the means we have
to employ."

No, Avery had not changed one whit; Charlie really
knew this when Avery became interested in Mitzie
Thompson.

Mitzie, like Charlie, was a freshman. She was one of
the first girls Charlie met when he came to the University
and it became Charlie's habit to wait for her after class,
to walk along with her between classes and to linger for
hours over coffee with her in the evening after the
library closed. One such evening, Avery approached
them, and sat with them at their table.

"I've been noticing Charlie's interest in you," he said
to Mitzie. "I'm glad he chose someone like you. Charlie's
one of my favorite people."

From that evening on, Mitzie and Avery were a pair.
A month later, they were pinned.

Charlie never forgot Mitzie—or the fact that he was in

love with her. He wrote about her—pages about her in his diary ("How gentle a thing is my love for her, and fragile, so that just to see her can suffice to start the rush of blood to my pulse and make my mind miss Mitzie, though she is across from me with someone else and all through me inside.") and he never walked a block in Columbia, Missouri, without being aware of how he would look to her should they meet; of what he would say; and in fantasy Charlie imagined their commune (he chose such a word for it), composed poems as though it had already happened and rehashed every brief conversation they had ever had, making more of it and improving upon it to such an extent that neither one would have recognized the other by the things that Charlie made them say.

"All right, Chazz." Avery stretched after he had copied the poem, and tossed the pencil and second sheet on the bed. "That does it now. I'll run along and see my Sheba. . . . Or should I say *yours*."

"Are you going to show it to her, Avery?"

"What do you think, Chazzy?"

As Avery left, he was singing:

> We've string beans and onions,
> Cabbage and scallions,
> But we have no bananas today . . .

MARCH 6, 1925

CHAPTER THREE

WHILE participating in a military maneuver over Kelly Field, Texas, on March the sixth, 1925, Charles Lindbergh was forced to abandon his plane and descend to earth by parachute, thus becoming automatically a mem-

ber of the select "Caterpillar Club" composed of aviators
forced to bail out while in flight.

On the evening of that same day, after participating
in a romantic maneuver of her own, which ended in her
being pinned to Otto Avery, Mitzie Thompson made
an entry in her five-year diary:

> Well, I did it. Neither one of us wanted it to hap-
> pen. Ave kept murmuring, "I have no right to do
> this, darling. No right . . . No right!" But it hap-
> pened anyway . . . How do I feel? Well, I don't
> know exactly, but I wasn't embarrassed at all about
> the wart the way I alway thought I'd be . . . .
> That's something!!! . . . When I got back to the
> sorority, the girls said, "What'd you and Ave do?"
> I told them: "Not much" . . . Not much! (ha! ha!).

Three months after that entry she wrote this:

> Sometimes I think all men are selfish. Lately it
> seems that more and more Ave doesn't care any-
> thing about me THAT WAY. I mean he cares,
> but only for his own pleasure. He says the reason
> I don't get anything out of it is I'm frigid, but I
> know better. DO I! . . . But men think they are the
> only one with feelings . . . I made an A in E-Lit
> again. Papa will be pleased.

Mitzie Thompson, in the beginning of her sophomore
year, was voted the girl with the most "It," and she was
still pinned to Otto Avery, though less and less did she
notice the fact he wasn't saying "I love you" as much as
he used to after their good-night kisses.

With Avery she was very comfortable, and sometimes
on week-end nights they didn't even bother making love
any more.

With Avery, she enjoyed a certain amount of freedom
which she somehow imagined made her a very blasé
young lady. During THAT TIME OF THE MONTH,
she quite nonchalantly mentioned that she had cramps,

and Avery, in turn, quite nonchalantly did little things to comfort her—offered aspirin; kissed her only on the forehead (as though it would be unholy under the circumstances to kiss her on the mouth) and frequently patted her tummy lightly and inquired: "Is my girl hurting?"

With Avery she was disenchanted at those times when she was sure he loved her more than she loved him; and enchanted when his eye strayed to another. But when he was behaving as he was on the evening of March 6, 1925, a few moments before he reached into his pocket and took out the poem Charlie Gibson had written, Mitzie was simply bored.

They were having coffee at a campus café across from the Administration building. Otto and Mitzie had been to an evening lecture on Hemingway, the new writer who had been causing such a stir lately, and subsequently inspiring everyone to talk in tough understatements out of the corners of their mouths. They had come into the café alone, and Mitzie had rather fancied they would take a table alone and indulge in a somewhat intense conversation centering on this Hemingway. She had been looking forward to it. For one thing she loved to picture herself holding intense conversations at a table alone with Avery, and to imagine people saying: "They must be awfully interesting, those two." And for another, she liked to listen to Avery's voice. It was fabulous; Avery was convinced radio was here to stay and he wanted to get a job in radio after he was graduated, so he was always practicing, imitating the announcers on the radio, and Mitzie liked to listen to him and fantasize herself *years* ahead, when someone would be exclaiming: "Oh, really! Why I hear him every evening. So you're Otto Avery's wife!"

But the moment after they had entered the café and put their coffees on a tray, Mitzie knew they wouldn't sit alone. She saw Avery's eyes become alert once he spotted two of his fraternity brothers at a table in the rear; and then he said in that snidely sly way of his—

whenever he thought he might amuse himself by being cruel: "Oh, look there! There's Fodor and O'Brien. Let's join *them*."

She knew too, even before they got to the table, that Avery would ride them, that he would begin again his annoying habit of teasing and ridiculing them in that ostensibly tolerant and amicable manner of his. He seemed to take some perverse pleasure in making buffoons of certain boys, and Fodor and O'Brien were among them.

Whenever Mitzie Thompson was bored, she flattened her short black flapper-cut hair to her pretty head by smoothing it over and over with the palm of her hand, and as she sipped her coffee beside Avery then, facing the two scapegoats he had chosen for the evening, she was doing just that.

"Whatever are you reading Fitzgerald for?" Avery was saying in his supercilious tone to the intimidated O'Brien, who was blushing down at a library copy of *The Beautiful and Damned*—"I wouldn't waste my time on him. He's not going to be at all important."

"I don't mind him," O'Brien managed.

"No, I suspect you don't. I suspect *you* think he's ripping. O'Brien, your tastes are so inconceivably mediocre. I wonder why you even try. Why *do* you try, O'Brien? Why?"

"Don't let him ride you, O'Brien," Mitzie had put in. "I like old Scotty myself. He suits me to a T."

O'Brien looked pleased, but Avery said, "It's all right for Mitz to think like that. Mitz is pretty. She can think any way she wants to because she's pretty. But you, O'Brien. *You're* not pretty, are you? Do you wish you were, O'Brien?"

"Why don't you stick to literature and stop getting personal," Fodor dared defend his colleague.

"Oh ho, so you're afraid we'll put things on a personal plane, eh, Fodor?" Avery grinned maliciously at Fodor. "Afraid we'll hurt little O'Brien's feelings, eh, Fodor? Well, I admire loyalty. In fact I've always admired the way you two stick together so much. Ever notice, Mitz, how these two stick together? They're inseparable, really. I mean, I'm not criticizing them, or insinuating anything. I mean it in the nicest way. Fodor and O'Brien. Just like Mister Gallagher and Mr. Shean—*in a way*, eh?"

"What the devil's the matter with you, Avery?" Fodor snapped.

"Oh, nothing with *me*." Avery chuckled.

So it went; and Mitzie sat and listened and smoothed her hair to her head and didn't listen. She daydreamed, and felt vaguely sorry for the two boys. Neither of them were Avery's match; otherwise he would never have picked on them; both were horrible bookworms, and rather weak, wilting types, suitable prey for Avery. Mitzie wished he wouldn't have the inclination to tease such types, but he did, and she would have to tolerate him because they were pinned. It was like being married.

Whenever her mind wandered from the conversation at the table, it seemed inevitably to drift back to a discussion she and Avery had had a week or so past. They had been talking about what they were going to do for Easter; and Avery was saying that the idea of going home bored him. He believed he'd go quail hunting with a group of the boys. Mitzie said that it would be nice, wouldn't it, if they could go off somewhere together, off to a hotel or something?

"What for?" He'd seemed surprised.

"Well, to be together."

"But *what for?* What would we do?"

"It's just that we never have been. Not overnight. We've always been in cars or woods or fraternity-house cellars."

"And what magic, pray, would be added to our relationship by the fact of a night spent surreptitiously in some hotel room?"

"We could—well, have breakfast together. We've never done that. We've never awakened together, Ave. It'd be —fun."

"Oh," Avery said, "I see. Then your idea of fun for

Easter is kissing one another's hung-over mouths every
morning, and afterward sipping orange juice atop
wrinkled sheets sprinkled with toast crumbs."

"You always spoil everything, Ave. I wish you
wouldn't."

"And I wish you'd grow up!"

It had been the closest they'd ever come to an argu-
ment—and that had been the only saving fact about it because Mitzie was worried at the fact they never seemed
to argue. Ave simply wouldn't. But it had hurt her quite
a lot more than she'd realized at the time, and she would
find herself dwelling on it in odd moments—and asking
her five-year diary: 1) Could he really love me if he
doesn't want me there in the morning? 2) Why does he
mock me whenever I'm a bit romantic? and 3) That
thing he said about hung-over mouths . . . It strikes
me he always drinks before we love! ! ! Why ? ? ? Or
should I just be glad he can get hootch. Ann K.'s boy
friend hardly ever can; and when he does, he always
gets sick. I couldn't stand it if Ave were ever to vomit.
Better count my lucky stars.

"Hey—" O'Brien eventually interrupted the conversation at the table— "there's Charlie Gibson coming in. Let's
hail him."

"Where?" Avery said, swinging around sharply to see.
"By God, *that* reminds me." He began to fumble frantically through his slicker pockets. "I have a little something here that'll be of interest to you, darling."

He nudged Mitzie, smiling, and then took out a piece
of folded yellow paper.

"I say, O'Brien," he said, "go and get Chazz; have him
join us. Only don't tell him *I'm* here. You see, it's his
birthday and I have a surprise planned for him."

O'Brien got up to go after Gibson, and Avery unfolded
the paper.

"Mitzie, listen to this. You too, Fodor. You're a scholar.
See what you think of this bit of poetry." He began to
read the lines slowly, forcing as much emotion into his
voice as he could:

Tell me how you like to see morning
Come for us. Say it sleepily—

Mitzie Thompson listened to it with some surprise, and Fodor frowned thoughtfully. But toward the end, as Avery was reading: "I love you when your arms hold me—" Charlie Gibson arrived at the table with O'Brien, and he stood stick-straight, staring, with his face beet red, and his coffee cup shaking.

"Ah, there you are, Chazzy," Avery said. "I was just reading your poem."

"Sit down," O'Brien said. "Aren't you going to sit down?"

Fodor said, "You write that, Gibson? Not bad."

"I think it's awfully good too," Mitzie Thompson said. "What's the matter?"

Charlie Gibson just stood there. He couldn't even look up from his coffee, or hold the cup still.

"It is good," Avery said expansively, "it's *very* good." He put his arm around Mitzie. "And do you know who it's written about?"

"Don't embarrass him, Ave. He has a right to a private life."

"But it's written to you, my darling. The title is *mitzie before breakfast.*"

At that, Charlie Gibson turned away abruptly, managed to walk four booths ahead and then sink down into the fifth, sitting like a stone with his back to them.

"Oh, Ave! Oh, gosh, that was *terrible!*"

"Of course." Avery spoke to Fodor and O'Brien now, "The amusing part of it is that Chazz boy has hardly had six words with Mitzie since he was a freshman. But you know he's in love with her. He's in love with her and he imagines—" Avery slapped the paper with the back of his hand— "this sort of thing."

"What an ass!" Fodor said, somewhat relieved that the spotlight had been turned on Gibson now.

O'Brien said, "Well, read it over. I didn't hear it all." And it was then and there, precisely at that moment,

that Mitzie Thompson felt a sudden surge of emotion
sweep through her; a very sad, tender, gentle emotion; an
emotion that made her, she thought, one with Dante's
Beatrice, Petrarch's Laura, and Tristram's Isolt; and besides, it had been called *mitzie before breakfast!* It had
mentioned awakening together, and for one solid year a
man had loved her without her knowing it. She, the girl
with the most "It," had inspired a poet. At Columbia,
Missouri, in the month of March in the year 1925, an incident had occurred which might well be recorded in the
literary annals of the future— "*. . . was reported that the
young poet was so shy in the presence of his beloved
that he fled—*"

"Where the devil are *you* going?" Otto Avery shouted
as Mitzie got up suddenly from the table.

"She's crying," O'Brien said.

"What's she crying about?" Fodor asked.

Otto Avery said, "She's being dramatic again." He
shrugged. "What's the date anyway? Probably her
period."

"It's the sixth," O'Brien said. "The sixth of March. Is
it really Charlie's birthday?"

And so, on Charlie Gibson's eighteenth birthday, Mitzie
Thompson ran weeping past him in the Ankle Inn Café,
and Charlie Gibson ran trembling after her.

In the street where he caught her by the arm, he
looked at his fingers clutching her coat, and then dropped
his hand from her as though he had touched a burning
coal. He blushed even more and said, "I'm sorry. I didn't
mean to—"

"That's all right," she said.

She blew her nose.

Charlie stood there.

She put the handkerchief back in her pocket. Neither
one knew what to say or where to go from there. A
group of boys and girls, their arms wound around one
another, feigning intoxication, staggered by singing bois-
trously, *Yes, We Have No Bananas.*

"Everybody's singing that dumb song," Charlie said, "but nobody I want to know is."

"Me too," she said. "Nobody I want to know is either."

With a common bond acknowledged, they began to walk along together—Mitzie Thompson and Charlie Gibson—she, on the verge of her second affair; he, still a virgin.

MARCH 6, 1957

CHAPTER FOUR

AFTER Charlie Gibson put aside the news clipping, he searched through his mail pile for the letter from his daughter, Jane (or Jayne, as she was now spelling it).

It was written on Radcliffe College stationery and it began quite simply:

Dear Dad,
I am having an affair . . .

Charlie felt his stomach do a flip. He gulped (he had been expecting "Happy Birthday" or something like that; never, *never* this), got a grip on himself and took a deep breath and exhaled as he continued to read:

with a man named Dudley Q. Davis, Harvard '59. At the risk of being labeled an exhibitionist by the fact that I announce this to you, I am going to state my reasons for so doing.
First of all, we're serious—*dead* serious. You and I are close, Dad, but we've never been very much alike. I guess I'm not very much like either you or mother. When I feel things, I feel them very, very deeply; and when I say that what I feel for Dud is more than love, far more, I wonder if you'll be able to understand. I ask you, please try!

Secondly, we're planning to go to Europe this summer, and that's another reason why I must make everything very clear to you. Dud's folks are comfortable, but they're not rich. For generations back, they've been Harvard; and their one wish is for Dud to be Harvard, too. It's a tradition I respect Dud for respecting.

If we were to do anything rash at this time (marriage) Dud would not be able to finish, and this would kill the Davises. I think you and Mom would like to see me finish Radcliffe, too.

Marriage is out!

Even if I were to use the money put aside for my education, to support Dud and I, his father would never forgive us if we were to marry before Dud got his B.A.

I don't want you to think Dud is one of these Ivy League types who places more importance on a "name" university than is justifiable. That isn't it at all; it's simply that there is tradition there and tradition *is* vital in human life.

Harvard, as far as Dud is concerned, is of very little consequence, outside of the tradition involved. And that brings me to our plans for Europe this summer . . .

You see, Dad, Dud is a writer. Notice that I don't say, "Dud wants to be a writer." He *is* one, and he's a very important one. In your business, Dad, you deal with hacks who sell emotions and ideals and rationale down the river for three cents a word—but Dud is not that kind of a writer. He's sensitive; and he's thoughtful; and he wants his work to live in aftertimes, to be read, and reread.

He's at work now on a series of poems, based along the idea of Pound's cantoes (Ezra Pound wrote poetry, poems called cantoes)—and it's his hope that in Europe this summer he'll perfect them. His folks are financing his trip, and I am going to ask you to finance mine.

Do you remember that you promised to buy me a car when I was graduated from Radcliffe? Instead of that, and now while I'm young and could make

real use of that money, in a more *real* way, I would
rather go to Europe with Dud.
I know you'll be shocked by this letter, Dad, and
angry too. But please try to appreciate the fact
that I'm not like you; I'm not even like the girls
you probably dated when you were in college.
Prudishness, false modesty, supercilious principles—
these things are archaic to me. I only know how I
feel. How deeply I feel. And for me, this feeling is
the only voice of reason.
I've seen Dud perspire, struggle, suffer anxiety
over, and weep because of a line of poetry he was
trying to make important. And I think this ex-
perience made me grow up and realize life has
to be meaningful—to me, to Dud, to people like us,
life has to have a message, something more than
the business world "step on toes and go for the
buck" philosophy; or the suburbia "wear comfortable shoes, read Dr. Spock, play Scrabble after
dinner" monotony.
Dad, I somehow know you won't fail me. You never
have, have you?
Please answer very soon.

> Best love,
> JAYNE

Charlie Gibson's first reaction to the letter was mute
shock, shock of the uncanny sort that seeps in on one
gradually, like water slowly flooding a leaky rowboat,
and he sat there at his desk momentarily in an effort
to get used to it. When he could—just barely—he seized
at the idea that his daughter did not mean "affair" in
the same sense as he had taken it. Not affair, *sexual,*
not that . . . Jane? . . . Jayne?

For some peculiar reason his mind shot back to a summer afternoon (how *many* years ago) when his wife
came out into the backyard, and pulled a lawn chair
up beside the hammock where Charlie was napping,
and said, "Well, Janie's finally gotten around to the
birds and bees."

"What do you mean?" Charlie woke up enough to

ask. Funny how he could recall too that he had stared up above his head at the caterpillar nests in the apple tree, and thought he ought to get a kerosene torch and burn them out of there. Funny how you could remember odd little things like that.

"Well," Joan had answered, "She asked me if women got babies kissing men."

"What'd you tell her?"

"She caught me off guard. I told her we'd have a long talk. I wanted to think about it first. About how to explain it."

"Good idea," Charlie had agreed. "We got any kerosene in the cellar?"

Had they ever had that long talk?

God, Charlie didn't even know. As much as he searched his mind, the only other memory he had along those lines was of an evening long after that day, when Janie was grown up, wearing spectator pumps and smoking cigarettes, and just lately being allowed a cocktail before dinner, along with Charlie and Joan. That evening, in a particularly jocular frame of mind (he had gotten a raise, hadn't he? They were celebrating something; or was it a final payment on the house?) he had mixed a second round of Manhattans, and Janie had gotten a little high. She had told a rather smutty story, more smutty than amusing, and Charlie had remembered that he had had some difficulty in laughing at it, though he *had* laughed, and that he had fought a sudden impulse to slap her mouth.

Later, when he and Joan discussed it, Joan had said, "Oh, kids always pick up the smuttiest kind of stories when they're growing up. I was a little appalled by it myself, until I remembered some of those *I* thought were clever when I was Janie's age . . . I wouldn't worry, darling. It's a phase."

Wasn't there any recollection in between that and this?

Any conceivable frame of reference for the casual announcement: *Dear Dad, I am having an affair?*

And of course after several slow seconds of semi-stupefaction, Charlie was forced to come to grips with the obvious—that it was an *affair* Jane meant. Not a crush, not an innocent romance, not even a collegiate "only from the waist up" passion—but an actual out-and-out "in bed" *affair*. One that he, Charlie, was expected to finance, in part, during its continuation this coming summer on the Continent.

"Like almighty hell I will," Charlie muttered to himself, "like almighty hell!" But as quickly as he had boiled with anger in that moment, he shrunk with that incredibly lost feeling of helplessness, thinking forlornly: Only what am I going to *do*? *What*? And, Janie, Janie, how did this *happen* to you?

The intercom on his desk was buzzing persistently; and finally he had to answer it; and monotonously, he had to dwell on his problem as he listened abstractedly to his secretary's voice, listened and wondered if *she* were having an affair, too, if she and all the bright-eyed, red-cheeked, soft-skinned, pretty little typists in the office pool were having affairs. And the receptionist, and girls (kids, really; babies) whom you passed on the streets of the city. You noticed they were cute, inhaled their perfumes, admired their legs, and then went by—never saw them again. Were they all having affairs? Or only Jane; only the Jaynes who studied Freud on ivy-infested campuses not too far from Boston and who somehow seemed to fathom the most minute facets of life by some process of osmosis?

". . . wants you to call her as soon as you can before lunch, Mr. Gibson," Bonnie was saying through the intercom, while Charlie was thinking: Good Lord, do you suppose Jane has a diaphragm?—not sure which was worse, the thought of her having one or the thought of her being without one.

"All right, I will," Charlie said. "I'll call her immediately."

"And Mr. Cadence says he'd really appreciate it if you could get the dummy up to him *before* four. He says the printers want to send a boy at five for the mock-up."

"Okay." Charlie sighed. *In your business, Dad, you deal with hacks who sell emotions and ideals and rationale down the river for three cents a word—but Dud is not that kind of—*

". . . guess that's all, Mr. Gibson, for the moment—except—have you read the memo yet?"

"Uh-uh . . . Not yet. I'm still working on my mail," Charlie answered.

MARCH 6, 1926

CHAPTER FIVE

IT WAS not only his nineteenth birthday—it was also his and Mitzie Thompson's first anniversary; and that whole year, they had waited.

Charlie did not want to take advantage of her, and Mitzie did not want to confess that he would not have been the first who had.

What puzzled Charlie most about *their* year, was that the two or three times when he had had too much hootch, and his hands had slipped and come very damn close to violating her inner sanctum, she had never reproached him—not *really* reproached him, but only whimpered ("whimpered like a frightened little puppy," Charlie had phrased it in his journal. "Gosh, I *am* a heel of the first water!"). And after, on "the next days" when Charlie could have kicked himself for being such a cur, Mitzie never mentioned it. And if *he* mentioned it, Mitzie always tacitly forgave him. That, Charlie decided, was because she loved him, and *that* invariably set Charlie to thinking: Gosh, did he love her as much as she loved him? I mean, I *love* Mitzie! But

she seems really to love me more; and I wonder if it's
fair to her to take up all her time without marrying
her.

What puzzled Mitzie most about *their* year, was that
Charlie *didn't* go any further; and she was alternately
torn between wondering whether the reason was that
he *couldn't,* and basking in the uncertain and unusual
glory of the fact that for one solid year she had been in
love with—and loved by—a boy who was six times as
passionate as any she had ever known ("All we do is
spoon," she had written in her five-year diary. "We
hardly even get around to moving pictures any more,
but just spoon. Wow, I'm not complaining, but—").
Yet he never forced the moment to its crisis. ("We
just simmer. We never boil.")

Once during *their* year, Charlie had said to her:
"Avery says he's been with you, you know. He's said it
three or four times around the house. Not in front of
me. I'd bust him for it. But he's said it."

"He's a liar!" Mitzie said flatly.

"Oh, gosh, don't I know that! He's always been a
liar."

But Avery was less of a problem during *their* year,
than Charlie had thought he would be. At first, Avery
pretended that instead of Charlie's having stolen Mitzie
from him, Avery had simply cast her off, and Charlie
was dating his hand-me-down. He made countless in-
nuendoes to that effect, but they were lost to most, who
knew the truth, and ignored by Charlie, who was far
too moonstruck to be bothered by them.

Then when spring came, three things happened which
distracted Avery. He went in training for baseball. He
tried out for and got the lead in *Beyond The Horizon,*
the new O'Neill play, which kept him in rehearsal for
months. And he began to concentrate considerable en-
ergy on riding a new boy—a DKE named Basescu who
had transferred from a New England university, a small
rather lithe young sophomore who was remarkably
brilliant and shy.

Their year was quite idyllic. In the summer when they separated, Charlie worked as a waiter at the Yacht Club up in his hometown in Auburn, New York. He wrote long letters late at night, *every night,* to Mitzie, and outlined a novel he was going to begin—already titled *Apostrophe*—about a man who turns away from the materialistic to the idealistic. (The dedication was written . . . "To Mitzie, whose feet contain no clay," with a question mark in the margin and a feasible second choice: "To Mitzie, who hath not feet of clay.")

Mitzie, in turn, lolled about under shade trees down in Bolivar, Missouri, wrote long letters which took her all day and which were constantly interrupted with such legends as: "10:30 A.M. just got up; 12 noon—after lunch; 4:30 P.M.—lying in the hammock;" and "saved herself" for Charlie by only dating on week ends.

When they were reunited in the fall, their magic persisted. Charlie wrote 410 poems about her. ("What I really want to do is experiment with poetry; is to learn, and introduce some new way of writing about this feeling I have for Mitz. I will yet!")

And Mitzie thought all 410 of them were beautiful; and they all made her cry. ("Otto Avery got some illness and hasn't returned to campus. They say he'll be out until after Christmas! . . . I'd be in some fix if I was still pinned to him! . . . Besides, Charlie is *IT*. There'll never be another, no matter what Papa says about being safer marrying lawyers or doctors—(ugh!")

When Charlie finally did find a new way to express his sentiments about Mitzie, he sent his experiment to a magazine. It read:

> Lines of an Inarticulate Fellow
> by Charles Kingsley Gibson
> *I want write about you!*
> *I want say things you like!*
> *I want you say ooh! ahh! ooh!*

The editors returned it with a comment: "Ugh!"

But the magic between Mitzie Thompson and Charlie Gibson still persisted; right up until March 6, 1926, approximately four minutes before March 7th of the same year.

Charlie knew he could wait no longer.

He had already come close to spoiling their record, with his urgency, three of four times during the week before the year was up.

After each time, he would force control on himself abruptly. He would hit his head with his fist, jump from the blanket spread out on the woods where they went for hikes, and groan: "Oh, gosh, Mitz, I'm a poor sort of pig, aren't I! Can't even wait out a year!"

"Don't feel bad," she'd tell him, in that funny little frail voice she always had during those interludes.

"But I do! I feel really rotten, Mitz. You ought to chuck me!"

But in the long run, despite the somewhat sloppy near-collapses of his standards, he *had* waited.

So he wanted it to be beautiful for them; he didn't want it to happen off in the woods or in a rumble seat or out on the frat-house lawn, but in a room; by candle-light, with music—and he'd buy a white rose to give her afterward.

It took planning, elaborate planning, because he didn't want it to seem planned. He figured a girl wouldn't want it to seem planned her first time. So he set about making arrangements.

The DKE's were giving a dance the evening of March 6; and this fact was decidedly in Charlie's favor. There would be empty rooms throughout the house. He had only to choose one which he knew for certain would remain empty right up until closing hour. That one would be Elliot Basescu's, the boy who had transferred from the New England college a year or so ago, the one whom Avery had picked for a scapegoat.

Basescu always went home to Kansas City for the week end when there were dances, and nobody could stand to room with Basescu because he never bathed, so Basescu had a single.

The position of Basescu's room was another point in Charlie's favor. It was right above the Chapter Room, where the DKE's held their meetings; and the Chapter Room was always empty and locked during dances, so that nobody below would hear any likely noises, were Charlie to choose Basescu's room.

It would be simple to get to the room, too; it could be gotten to by a back staircase, right off of the kitchen. It was the first one on the right at the top.

All Charlie had to do was check the facts.

"Of course I'm going for the week end." Basescu peered up sullenly from a copy of *The Forsyte Saga.* "Since when is it *your* concern?"

"How about lending me your key?"

"Why on earth should I?"

"Well . . ." Charlie decided to come right out with it. "I want to bring a girl up, Basescu. I'll pay you."

"How much?" Basescu was a notorious miser. He'd do anything for money, everyone swore.

"Two dollars," Charlie said.

Basescu said, "Three."

"Two and a half. That's final!"

"Three," Basescu said.

Charlie said, "All right, Basescu. Three!"

He slapped the bills down and Basescu reached a puny hand out and grabbed them. Charlie noticed the dirt encrusted under Basescu's fingernails. He decided he'd have to sneak up on the afternoon of the dance and put his own clean linens on Basescu's bed.

"And keep your mouth shut about it, too!" Charlie said as he walked out of the room. "You can leave the key in my mailbox when you take off."

Basescu only grunted.

Charlie was beginning to feel somewhat lightheaded then, when he collided with Avery on his way down the frat-house stairs. Since Avery's ulcer attack, he had returned to college with less enthusiasm for vituperative scenes and a somewhat more sullen, if not somber, outlook. He even went easy where Basescu was concerned, and was almost friendly, at times, with Basescu. But they still had bitter outbreaks from time to time, usually incited by Avery, who on occasion could not resist riding Basescu about his money-hunger.

Toward Charlie, though, Avery was simply grudging —not in the sly, smiling, malicious way of the past, but more coldly disdainful. Charlie believed he still carried the grudge of Mitzie's disloyalty, but Charlie didn't care any more what Avery felt. He didn't even mind what Avery said to him when they collided there on the stairs.

"Well, well, Chazz . . . you still going with Easy Mitzie?"

"Still green about it, Avery?"

"She *is* easy, Chazz. Easy to *know*, in the Biblical sense of the word."

"Take care of your ulcer, old man." Charlie laughed and waved, and then ran on.

Avery shouted after him: "I could prove it, Chazz!"

Everything went smoothly in the beginning.

At supper that night, the DKE's rose as a corps and sang: *It's His Birthday, He's A Sport!* to an excited Charlie, who sat thinking: I'm not going to rush things with her. Gosh, we'll even sit around for a while just talking beforehand. Maybe sit around in the nude.

Basescu left the key as planned; and that afternoon Charlie had sneaked up and fixed his linen on the bed, put the rose in water outside the window and hid a candle in the desk drawer. He'd even managed to get a scratchy recording of Ravel's *Daphnis et Chloë* from someone in the house, and a phonograph.

By nine o'clock, when the DKE's were heading out to pick up their dates, Charlie had checked twice on everything. Then he put his overcoat on and set off to get Mitzie.

Two hours later he was gently guiding her through

the kitchen, up the back stairs and into Basescu's room.

"Isn't this a swell idea!" Charlie exclaimed nervously as they settled side by side on the old leather couch in the foreroom, just in front of the cubicle that contained Basescu's bed. Charlie lit the candle and looked hungrily at her. She was wearing a green net gown, and off in the bowels of the DKE house a chorus of inebriated coeds were singing:

C'lle-giate, c'lle-giate. Yes! we are collegiate!
Nothing in-ter-med-jate, No, ma'am!

"It's a swell idea, all right," Mitzie said.

"It's quiet," Charlie said. "That's what I like about it."

"I like the candlelight."

"Oh, gosh, yes, I do too."

"And it's quiet. . . So this is where you boys live, huh?"

Regardez le maison de ce garçon," Charlie said. Mitzie giggled appreciatively.

They were silent then. Charlie reached for her hand and squeezed it.

Trousers baggy and our clothes look raggy,
Hot Dog!
Garters are the things we never wear. . .

"I just de-*test* that awful song," Mitzie said. "Honestly, I can't stand it."

"I know it."

"The old songs were awfully good, but I just can't stand the new ones."

"They're awful," Charlie said, playing with her little finger. "Remember *Kiss In The Dark?* That was a *song!*"

"And *Blue Moon.*"

"And *Margie.*"

" And *Three O'clock In The Morning,*" Mitzie said, beginning to sing: *"It's three o'clock in the morn-ning—"*

With Charlie joining in:

We danced the whole night through.
It's three o'clock in the morn-ning—
Mmm-hmm-hum-hum-hum-hmm—

"I don't know the words," Mitzie said. "Only those first few lines."

Charlie said huskily: "I love you."

"Oh gosh; gosh, so do I."

Then he took her in his arms, thinking: Should I tell her, or just sort of naturally let us find our way into the next room after we spoon awhile? Wonder what time it is, anyhow?

Fifteen minutes later they had "just sort of naturally" found their way into the next room, because Mitzie had said she was always curious about frat men's bedrooms: "I always sort of picture them sleeping on old cots or something, like in the army," she had said.

"Oh, gosh, no. No, *real beds*. C'mere and look."

Then they got comfortable.

"I mean we're no more indecent now than if we were on a beach going swimming," Mitzie said. "I mean I don't wear any more than this on a beach going swimming."

"I don't either," Charlie said. "Want me to put music on?"

They played the record of *Daphnis et Chloë* twice, and during the third time, Charlie said: "I like Ravel. What's that there, anyway?"

"Ravel was never my forte," Mitzie said. "What's what?"

"Where my hand is?"

"Oh, that," Mitzie said. "It's a wart. . . . I like Mendelssohn."

"It's a funny place for one," Charlie whispered.

Then after he kissed her for a long time, he said, "Gee!"

"What?"

"Gee, I just thought of a poem."

"What poem?"

"No, I mean, I just wrote one—in my mind. I'll call it: *Conversation While Listening to Daphnis and Chloë.* Here's the way it goes:

> "*No, Ravel is not my forte.*
> *What's that there, is that a wart?*
> *That's a funny place for one.*
> *But I'm fond of Mendelssohn.*"

Charlie chuckled. "We'd be the only ones who'd appreciate it."

She was quiet for a few seconds. Then she said: "Thanks, Charlie."

"For the poem?" He was surprised; she sounded very solemn.

"I used to feel sensitive. I mean, about the wart."

"Huh? What's the matter with it? I like it!"

"No, wait a minute. I really used to be sensitive about it. When I was a kid I used to think I'd never get married because I wouldn't want anyone to know about—having a wart there. It used to bother me. You don't know!"

"Well, gosh, I didn't mean to make fun of it. I think it's swell."

"Oh, I'm not mad, Charlie. That's just it. You make it seem so—natural. I mean, I never even talked about it before with anyone . . . I just—think—well, gee, Charlie —gee—"

"Aw, gee, Mitzie," Charlie murmured, crushing himself to her, "gee, baby, oh g-gosh——"

Ten minutes after the dream had begun it became a nightmare.

Neither one of them were aware of the persistent clicking of the needle of the phonograph as it played endlessly in the final groove; and for the same reason, neither heard the turn of the key in the lock.

What was heard was a rowdy chorus bellowing:

Happy birthday to you
Happy birthday to you
Happy birthday, dear—

And by that time, Charlie had leaped from Basescu's bed and stood white with shock, facing a dozen of his fraternity brothers, their faces in shadows. Otto Avery stood in the foreground, holding a cake resplendent with nineteen candles. Mitzie, of course, had screamed, then pulled the sheet up over her head.

"Surprise!" Avery said, grinning. "A surprise for our Chazz!"

Behind him, the other boys stood as shamefully embarrassed as Charlie, for they suddenly realized the sort of situation upon which they had intruded. It was obvious that only Avery knew the malicious surprise which was masked with the innocent one.

There were mumblings:

"Sorry, Charlie."

"God, fella, we didn't know."

"Avery, you're a rotten bastard."

"We'll clear out, Charlie. God!"

None of them saw behind Charlie into Basescu's cubicle, but all of them knew it was Mitzie Thompson's quivering form folded humiliated in the bed linen, and all of them got out as quickly as they were able.

Avery set the cake on Basescu's couch.

He had the familiar snide smirk on his mouth as he turned to leave; and for his parting words, he said, "Many happy returns, Chazz boy. What'd Mitz give you, eh? Couldn't have been a wart."

Then he slammed the door.

Downstairs, the dance was still going on. The orchestra was playing *Just a Cottage Small by a Waterfall*, and in the kitchen, a group was competing with:

You can bring Pearl,
She's a darn nice girl,
But don't bring Lulu—

Upstairs, *Daphnis et Chloë* was still spinning endlessly around the turntable of the phonograph; but its music was gone.

Mitzie Thompson put her clothes on wordlessly; and Charlie Gibson stood in the other room, smoking a cigarette and staring out at the night, in his underwear, with his back to the birthday cake.

MARCH 6, 1957

CHAPTER SIX

EVERYBODY at Cadence Publications knew the story about Marge Mann, and the spike on Wally Keene's desk.

The stunt was a typical Keene one—one of his "psychological" ones.

He left a railroad spike out on his desk, near the edge of a corner, so that whoever came into his office was tempted, as he talked with Keene, to touch it, pick it up, or fondle it, in the abstract way of preoccupied people.

The first day he put it there, he invited one of the men from Circulation to come down to his office; and on sundry pretexts, he asked practically every female executive in Cadence to come in for a chat. Then, both men would observe the woman's reaction to the railroad spike. In Keene's words: "The thing was so goddam phallic, it was bound to be revealing!"

There was Miss Novick, for example, a prissy, pursemouthed production chief on the shelter magazine, *Your Home.* As she talked with Keene, her fingers barely skirted along an edge of the spike; skirted there, then gingerly were withdrawn.

Miss Bonner, the beautiful young fashion editor on

that magazine, picked up the spike and lovingly caressed it throughout her conversation with Keene.

Miss Angelo, Keene's pretty and sweet nineteen-year-old secretary, picked it up, looked at it, then gently put it back in its place.

There were various "revealing" reactions on the part of the female employees toward Keene's phallic symbol, but the one reaction no one ever forgot—and Wally Keene never forgave—was the reaction of Marge Mann.

At first, she picked it up without particularly noticing it, and she stood gripping it for a few seconds. Next, with rather roughshod enthusiasm, she began tossing the spike from hand to hand. Then finally, at a pause in the conversation, she noticed the spike in her hands. She looked at it, looked at Keene, and before tossing it with a thud to the desk, she said, "What the hell do you need this old thing for?"

"Penis envy," Wally Keene had said about it. "She has a chronic case. God, did you see the way she threw the thing on the desk!"

And everyone who heard the story laughed and agreed, and it became a standard. Even Marge herself said later, "Well, if the goddam spike had been on anyone else's desk, I might not have had the same reaction . . . But *Wally Keene!* After all!"

For from the beginning, they had felt a relentless antipathy toward one another.

Marge was a woman whom most men liked—liked in the "pal" sense. They got a kick out of her, they could tell their most obscene stories without any qualm, and could count on her consistently for an ear that was *simpatico* about anything from their bleeding ulcers to their wives' post-partum depression periods. Marge was "a good kid," "a real swell gal," and "a helluva sport!"

Only two men who worked with Marge at Cadence had felt differently toward her from the general male. They were Keene and Charlie Gibson.

Keene had hated her. Charlie had loved her.

On the morning of March 6, 1957, Marge Mann sat

idly over a copy of the *Times*, pretending to read it, and trying to keep from thinking of either of these men.

But she would no sooner read: "Paul M. Butler denounced tonight Eisenhower Administration claims of civil rights achievements as—" than she would begin to worry: Why doesn't Charlie call me back? I've called him twice. In the elevator this morning—he looked as though he knew something. Why doesn't he call me back?

And she would no sooner force her eyes back to the *Times* and read: "From London came news of new friction in Parliament over the matter of—" than she would cry within herself, God, why did I beg Keene the other night? God, *why?*

It had happened in a sudden, compulsive way—the whole thing; from her picking up the telephone and inviting Keene over to her place for drinks, to hearing her door slam hours later, hearing his nonchalant whistling outside in the hall as he punched the elevator button, and lying in the dark—hungry, with the taste of Scotch in her mouth; naked, and staring across the room at the tropical fish swimming in their lighted tank; the feeling of being old; too old now to do anything about the fact she had of being old; too old now to do anything about the fact she'd fouled her life up good.

It had happened after lunch—the phone call she had made. In a sense it had happened because of what had transpired over the fruit salads and whisky sours in Michael's Pub, between Blance Phelan and herself.

Blance was an old friend of Marge's. They'd been in publishing together for years. Before Blance took her present job as an executive editor on the new home magazine Dorset Publications was sponsoring, Blance had held a job similar to Marge's—a job as homemaking editor on a women's slick magazine. They'd often had lunch and drinks together, gone to meetings and parties, and gone to movies and the theater. About fifteen years they'd known one another, and they could talk freely, frankly.

Blance said, "Do you think you *ought* to have another drink, Marge?"

"My God, it'll only be my fourth. That's a funny thing for you to say, Blance."

"Well, I just wonder if you should."

"When did you start this drink-counting business?"

"Marge, things aren't going well for you, are they?"

"I've got bills, if that's what you mean. My operation was goddam expensive, but you know me. I don't let it get me down."

"And the job?"

"Same as ever."

"Really?"

"No, not really . . . Not the same at all. There's a slight personality difference between me and some young punk Cadence hired."

"And that's all it is?"

"That's all! Where's my drink, anyway?"

"I wish you wouldn't have it, Marge. You know when you're faced with a problem, drinking just makes good things bad and bad things worse."

Marge chuckled and winked at Blance. "A little philosophy is all I need, eh? . . . Aw, Blance, you know me. I can roll with the punch . . . I might even leave Cadence . . . might start sending out feelers, letting people know I'm available . . . Don't know why I owe Cadence any loyalty. What's the situation over at Dorset? Could you use a high-priced homemaking editor?"

"Do you want me to tell you the truth, Marge?"

"Why not, honey? But I want my drink more."

"He's bringing it . . . Listen, Marge, you're getting a bad name. Marge, I'm no prude. I'm pretty realistic, and I know you, Marge. I know when you're in trouble. Other people don't have to tell me, either. I know the way you behave, the way you joke; the flip act you put on."

"So people are talking. People always did."

"Marge, a woman in our field can't afford to get a reputation as a lush."

"Oh, honey, I was always a maverick in our field. Where the hell I ever got the notion to major in home economics, I'll never know! But I did, and I know my stuff. And if I tell a dirty joke every now and then around my illustrious colleagues, it doesn't matter a goddam, because I know my stuff!"

"No one's indispensible, Marge—least of all, women our age."

"Blance, let me tell you something. Before I went to Cadence, in the photographs for the homemaking sections, the models would be wearing Bergdorf Goodman sheaths and emerald clips from Van Cleef and Arpels, and they'd be mixing up cake batters in some fabulous Frank Lloyd Wright kitchen of the future. That was how Cadence was going about wooing a mass audience. They knew less about reader identification than a lecturer at the Frick Museum knows about pushing dope . . . *I* had to tell them. And I did tell them. A few times I even went to the five-and-ten myself to get props for the photographs, to get a housedress for the model to wear, or a set of those plastic cannisters for the picture, so that the readers could look at our magazines and see *themselves*—not some ultra-sophisticated slant-eyed model from the Plaza Five Agency, but themselves, and their neighbors next door . . . Don't tell me I wasn't indispensible to Cadence, Blance!"

"I'm not talking about then, Marge. I'm talking about *now*."

"And, Blance, listen, when I came to Cadence you should have seen the way they gave the recipes. It never occurred to them that the poor ninny out way to hell and gone in Ida Grove, Iowa, bent over some hot-as-hell stove, would like the ingredients listed in the order that they are to be added to the dish. They never even thought of trying to make it easy for the reader, and as a matter of fact, before I came to Cadence, they didn't have a test kitchen. They didn't even test the recipes sometimes. Just shoved them into the magazines without testing them. I could use another drink; get his eye . . . I had to fight for that kitchen."

"I'm not even getting through to you, am I, Marge?"

"Oh, you're coming in fine, baby. It's just that I don't think you realize how indispensible I was to Cadence. Every single appliance in that test kitchen, *I* got for Cadence, for *nothing*. Gratis, I got it, Blance. Just because it never before occurred to Cadence that the manufacturer would be getting thousands of dollars of advertising free by the very fact we shot our food pictures in the kitchen, and all the stoves and refrigerators and electric mixers and what-the-hell else would show in the pictures. They were glad to equip our test kitchen free. Glad, hell, they were *grateful* . . . Where's my drink? This place is getting too popular lately."

"Marge," Blance said quietly, "you're shouting. You're saying very obvious things; and you're getting tight. Try to keep from being afraid. If you can keep from being afraid, you can lick this, Marge. Do you hear me?"

"Yes," Marge Mann had answered, suddenly aware of how she must have sounded, of the meaning of the words she had been saying, of what was happening to her. She sat for a moment, then clutched at a cigarette and let Blance light it. Then she said, "Blance, I think they're going to demote me . . . If they do, I'll have to quit. They know I will; that's why they'll do it. I'll have to resign, Blance . . . And I'm sixty years old."

"You can still do something about it, can't you?"

"I'm sixty years old. I have nothing in savings; and I have less than five hundred dollars still in stocks. I'm really sitting pretty, aren't I?"

"Why don't you try to do something about it, Marge?"

"What can I do about a young punk who hates my guts and who's the fair-haired boy at Cadence?"

"Can't you talk with him?"

"No. What the hell would we talk about. About poor little old me and please be kind?"

"Just try to talk rationally with him. Tell him you'd

like to work with him—not at cross purposes. Bury the hatchet."

"Oh, God, you don't know him, Blance."

Hours later, after Marge had gone back to Cadence and quite impulsively picked up the interoffice phone and called Wally and asked him if he'd like a drink at her place, she had suddenly realized that *she* didn't know him either.

She didn't know him; and she didn't know what she was going to say to him when he walked in her door at six o'clock.

But when it happened, her feelings didn't show. She opened the door with a flourish and a pitcher of Martinis in one hand; and she said, "Hi, fella, could you use a Martini?"

"Hello, Marge," Wally Keene answered calmly. He strolled in and glanced about the apartment in an abstract manner. "I see you've already had a few. Is that why you wanted to come home first, so you could have a few before I came?"

She laughed as though he were making a joke, hating his superior air, the neat, young, handsome look of him—the two-years-out-of-Yale look, and the young-man-on-his-way-up-*in-a-hurry* look.

"As a matter of fact," she said, "I wanted to straighten up a little. My maid's gone South for the winter."

"Nice place," he said. "I'd always heard these Southgate Apartments were very chic. Is that a Degas on the wall?"

"Yes."

"Nice."

"Thanks . . . Want a Martini, Wally?" Feeling a little more sure now. "Hmm?"

"Okay, Marge," he answered, placing his coat on the couch. "You have a nice view too. High up; looking out at the city, eh?"

"I like it," she said.

For half an hour or so, it went easy like that. They sat side by side on the semicircle-shaped velvet couch before the fireplace, their drinks set on the kidney-shaped, marble-top coffee table. The apartment was a pleasant one—a big one, though it was only one large room with a small kitchen and foyer off to one side and a small dressing room and bath off to the other. But it looked big, and somehow plush. Marge was extravagant and flamboyant; and it looked like the kind of place she would live in, the kind of place someone would go to for cocktails in Manhattan, and think, *this* is nice.

Marge Mann didn't look sixty certainly. She seemed younger—vivacious, amusing, pretty. Sometimes people mistook her for Wendy Barrie—that always pleased her —sometimes, for Eve Arden.

As she sat beside Wally, drinking—on her fifth—she began to think Blance was right; all she had to do with Wally was bury the hatchet, be friendly; and she noticed how easily they conversed and she felt glad she had gotten the impulse to ask him here. She laughed when he said: "You know, Marge, the only thing that's somewhat incongruous here is that fish tank!"

"My poor fishies," she responded gaily. "They're so pretty. Sometimes at night I just turn the lights out and sit here in the dark and watch them. I just love to watch them, all the colors. Want another drink? *I* do . . . Poor fishies."

"I've still got some."

"You're slow, eh, Mr. Keene?" She smiled at him, reaching for the pitcher. "Gee, I just thought. Mr. Keene, tracer of lost persons . . . Remember that radio program?"

"Um-hmm . . . You drink quite fast, don't you?"

"I've always been a heavy drinker, I guess. I couldn't wake up in the morning without my little old can of beer."

"Really? You drink in the morning?"

"Well, look papa-doodle," Marge Mann said, feeling very lightheaded and happy by now, "I don't make like an alky or anything. I just like my little old can of beer."

"Where'd you pick up that expression?"

"Which one, papa-doodle?"

"*That* one!"

"Oh, I always say that when I'm happy. Papa-doodle. Don't know where it came from. Like it?"

"Un-uh."

"Scuse me, papa-doodle."

"I think you're getting crocked, Marge."

"Who's crocked? I'm a little high, papa-doodle, but I'm as sober as you."

Keene looked at her, disgust evident in his facial expression. Then he studied his glass, and finally, "What do you want, Marge?"

"What does who want?"

"Look, don't play around. You want something. You asked me up here for a reason. Before you get too crocked, and before I have to catch my train, why don't you tell me."

"Okay, papa-doodle," she said. "I will. I asked you up here to bury the hatchet."

"Oh?"

"There's no sense working at cross-purposes, is there, papa-doodle? We both work at Cadence, so we might as well get along."

"I wish you'd stop using that expression. It's nauseating."

" 'Scuse, 'scuse, 'scuse . . . a thousand pardons . . . Want another drink?"

"I'm still working on this one."

"Well, I'll have one before all that ice melts and turns it into water." She reached for the pitcher, and knocked a cigarette to the floor. She fumbled to find it, lurched a little against the table, recovered the cigarette and poured herself a seventh Martini.

"Love these," she said.

Wally Keene said, "Look, Marge, I'll put my cards on the table."

"Okay, papa-doodle."

"As far as I'm concerned you're not right for the job you have. Bruce hired me as a troubleshooter. That's not my fault. That's my job; and part of my job is to decide what's best for Cadence—and to be perfectly frank and honest about it to Bruce."

"And I ain't best for Cadence, huh, papa-doodle?"

He gave her an exasperated glance. "You really go all to pieces when you drink, don't you? You forget how to talk. Your hair starts getting wispy; you really sort of go to pieces—with this "ain't" and "papa-doodle." You really regress, don't you?"

"Regress?"

"Become infantile. Like a baby."

"You and your psychology, papa-doodle. You and your lousy psychoanalysis. If you're a troubleshooter, papa-doodle, whyn't you shoot for the trouble that's the trouble with you, 'stead of running to a head-shrinker, papa-doodle?"

"You drink to make people sorry for you. You just become helpless, don't you, Marge, like a baby—to make people feel they have to take care of you."

"If I make people feel that way, 'n why in hell do you want to try and get me demoted, if I make people have to take care of me?"

"You're awfully drunk. There isn't much point in talking with you."

"Papa-doodle ain't going to be friends with Margie?"

"Papa-doodle couldn't care less. Besides, I have a train to catch at the moment." He set his drink down on the marble-top table with an empathic gesture.

She grabbed his sleeve. "Wally?" she said. "Why don't you like me? You didn't from the start, papa-doodle. Why not?"

"I had no feelings about you personally whatsoever. I just knew that, objectively, you weren't right for the job."

"Aw, no, papa-doodle, you didn't like me. You didn't. What'd I do, huh? What can I do to make you like me, Mr. Keene?"

"Christ, you're a lush! You're not a very pleasant lush, either. You're an *old* lush."

"Ah ha, so! Now we hear, hah, papa-doodle. I'm old lush, hah? Well, you wait. Now, you wait." She pulled herself to her feet, pointing a finger at him. "Now, you wait. You wait." She walked into the foyer, passing the bar there. She stopped and thought aloud, mumbling: "Didn't come in *here*. Went into the dressing room. Whoops, did so come in here. Mistake. This ain't the dressing room, mamma-doodle. This here's the bar . . . Whoops. Got to go back." She stared at a bottle of J. & B., grinned foolishly, and grabbed it by the neck after unscrewing the cap in a careful, studied way. Then she raised it to her lips, letting the Scotch pour down her throat.

From the other room, Keene shouted: "What are you doing, anyway? You're not fixing yourself another drink, for the love of God?"

"Just you wait," she said. "Now, I'm coming right out there."

She appeared, wearing the same silly grin. This time she walked to the couch opposite the one where Keene was sitting. With effort, she pulled off first one pillow, then the other.

Keene said, "What the hell are you doing?" and got up, his eyes angry.

"Well, papa-doodle, I'm pulling down my bed is what. I'm pulling down the bed that only a child can work. You seen 'em advertised on TV, papa-doodle."

"Here—" Keene tried to help, but the bed came crashing out and down, the mattress covered with crumpled white sheets.

Keene said, "Yeah, go on to bed and sleep it off. Best idea you've had all night."

"Wait," she said, "just wait," and she staggered off across the room to the dressing room. Then she slammed the door.

Keene started for his coat.

She shouted: "Don't leave, now; just wait."

He was uncertain of what to do. He thought maybe he ought to wait until she fell into the bed; once she did that, she'd surely pass out. He thought: God damn her anyway.

She squealed: "I'm coming out, papa-doodle. In a minute. And I ain't just whistlin' Dixie, papa-doodle."

Keene hit his head with his palm. *God Almighty!*

Then he looked up and saw her.

"Old lush, hah?" she said, standing there, naked, running her hands over her naked body. It was a mature woman's naked body, with the huge hips and pendulous breasts; the great white thighs; the body of a woman no longer young, but female—female and somehow very pale and too soft, with slight stretch marks—those slight wrinkles which Keene had never seen on a woman because he had never seen a woman who was old standing naked before him. "Old lush, hah? Ever see a body like this on an old lush? I got a good body. A *young* good body." Her hands ran down her flesh, up again. She kept smiling in that silly way.

She said, "Surprised, aren't you?"

He began to feel sick, repulsed and sick inside. "I have a train to catch," he said. "I'm going now."

"I can tell by your face, papa-doodle," she said, walking to the bed. "You're getting that weak-in-the-knees feeling, aren't you, papa-doodle? You didn't expect your mamma to come across like this, hah? And you're a scared little boy, hah? You want me, don't you, papa-doodle? You want me."

He stood staring at her; staring incredulously as though he were watching some bizarre and hideous something which he didn't quite understand, and knew only that it was there. *He* was there with it, listening to it, a witness to the sad and pitiful and awful exposure of the preposterous proportions of the human ego, a witness to a person's tragically deceived self-concept. And it made him hate her that he had to bear witness.

But he stood, almost as though transfixed; stood those slow seconds and watched her stretch her naked woman's

body on those wrinkled sheets. He watched her trying to
force some semblance of remembered coyness to the
features of her face and heard her say in the bygone
voice of another time's seduction: "Take me. You can
have what you want."

Wally Keene turned, took up his coat and without
looking back at her, he snapped the light button off,
opened the door and walked out of her apartment.

In the hallway he punched the elevator button frantically. He was shaking, and he began to whistle; he
began to whistle *I Want a Gal Just Like The Gal That
Married Dear Old Dad* and kept it up until he stepped
into the little box and rode down. Then, when he realized it, he felt a surge of nausea, and knew that his
hour on Dr. Mannerheim's couch the next day would
be an agonizing one. He tried (to keep from actually
being nauseated) to concentrate on something frivolous
and unimportant—his home in Greenwich, Mary and
the kids.

And in the darkness, back on the fifteenth floor, Marge
Mann began to moan, began to moan in the manner of
the member of a Greek chorus mourning death.

Once again that morning, Marge Mann forced her eyes
back to the *Times*, back to ". . . . on another political
front, the Secretary of the Interior chose Senator—"
until what always seems like a miracle to a person waiting for a phone to ring, happened: the phone rang. And
Charlie Gibson said, "Hi, there. I would have called you
sooner, but something's happened that's really shaken
me up."

Marge felt the sinking sensation in her stomach, and
thought, Here it comes . . .

". . . can't seem to believe it," Charlie was saying. "I
think you'll find it hard to believe, too."

"Okay," Marge said. "Fire away."

"Well, maybe we can have lunch. Are you free?"

"I'll *get* free. . . . Charlie?"

"Yeah?"

"Is it real bad news?"

"It's pretty serious," Charlie Gibson answered. "It's about Jane."

MARCH 6, 1939

CHAPTER SEVEN

AT thirty-two, Charlie Gibson was still writing poetry.

Mitzie Thompson had long since been forgotten and Charlie had been married for three years to Joan Quigly, a girl he had gone to school with back in Auburn, New York. He was the father of a two-year-old daughter; they had an apartment on Central Park West, which cost a little more than they could afford, and Charlie was employed as an assistant editor at Cadence. He was, everybody said, Bruce Cadence's new fair-haired boy.

Charlie wasn't writing a lot of poetry; just every now and then, and only for one person—Marge Mann.

On the afternoon of his thirty-second birthday, immediately after lunching at The Lambs' Club with Bruce, Charlie did two things, which more or less explained his predicament in life at that time.

First, he stopped at a florist and arranged to have three yellow roses sent to Marge c/o Cadence. Then, from a piece of scratch paper, he copied a poem he had composed that morning, onto a card to be enclosed.

On the envelope of the card he wrote, "5:15 at the 50th Street entrance to Saks."

The card itself read:

Wear a hat with a feather on it and walk
Like a duchess stepping over the bodies of serfs
In your blond-laughing look and dearest talk

*Stand by the counter where they sell men's hats
And wait for me, though I'll be early.*

The next thing Charlie did was to cross the street to a drugstore, call his wife in the phone booth, and tell her he would be quite late.

"How late?" she wanted to know. "Charlie, it's your birthday. I—"

"I know it's my birthday. I *know* that! This is business."

"But how late? I've planned dinner. You're not going to miss dinner?"

"All right, I'm not going to miss dinner. But it'll be late. Nine or ten o'clock."

"Oh, Charlie."

"Well, you can have a sandwich or something before, can't you?"

"I guess I'll have to."

"I've got a right to be late on my own birthday, haven't I?" Charlie Gibson said inanely; then added quickly, "It's important business."

"Wait a minute," Joan answered. "Can you hear her, Charlie? Listen . . . could you hear that? . . . Hear, Charlie? She's cooing at you . . . say dada, Janie."

When Charlie Gibson finally did wait by the counter where they sell men's hats, at the 50th Street entrance to Saks that afternoon, he was still brooding over the phone call, still hearing his daughter's sounds, still resenting the fact that Joan had held Janie to the phone so that he could hear her—as though Joan were reprimanding him in some subtle way, by reminding him they were married people now, with responsibility; *responsibilities!* Of course it was silly for Charlie to think it was an insidious bit of strategy on Joan's part; but it helped to think it was; and in the unreasonable manner of someone searching for an excuse, for some salve to alleviate the burden of guilt this affair with Marge was inflicting upon him, Charlie began to gripe: Well, what if I really did have an important business appointment tonight? That would have been a hell of a tactless maneuver; first, complain-

ing because I'm going to be a little late; then forcing
our daughter to gurgle into the receiver as though I
were deserting them to go to China! You'd think a wife
would be more sensitive to her husband's feelings . . .
What the hell, she doesn't know anything about Marge.
For all Joan knows, it is business . . . It was a damn
unnecessary thing to do. Typical!

"When did you start talking to yourself, darling?" a
voice said behind him. He whirled and saw Marge
smiling at him—tall, beautiful, flamboyant Marge, with
the boa furs strung over her shoulders; the Femme she
always wore, giving the excitement of its scent to Charlie; and the red hat with the feather bobbing dizzily off
to the side. He saw her and thought: Beautiful bitch;
and thought: Smart, sophisticated Marge. He marveled
a little at how enchanting she always looked, and then
at the fact he was with her—all of this in the few seconds it took for them to touch hands, and for Charlie
to say: "Was I honestly talking out loud?"

"No, but your lips were moving. I walked right past
you, looked right at you. You didn't even see me."

"Unlikely."

"No, it's true . . . I loved the poem, darling. The roses.
I love you."

"Did you finish your shopping?"

"I only had one thing to get. Something for you. But
I'm not going to give it to you here."

"How about the Gotham? Feel like a drink?"

"The Gotham . . . I wore a feather."

"I noticed."

"Is something the matter, Charlie?"

"I could use a drink. That's all."

The Gotham was crowded. It was a bad choice; they
were crowded between two couples on either side, and
it was noisy.

Marge said, "Let's not even order. We can cab to my
place."

"Might as well have one here."

"You *are* going to take me to dinner, darling?"

"I said I would."

"Thanks, Charlie . . . thanks."

"I didn't mean it that way."

"Just remember, *I* didn't make the date for tonight. I knew she'd want you home tonight. Remember that."

"It hasn't got anything to do with her."

"Then what has it got to do with? Everything went all right with Bruce, didn't it? Did you suggest the blurbs under the titles on the contents page?"

"I did."

"Well, he liked it, didn't he?"

"He always likes *your* ideas, Marge. That's why he likes me."

"Order me a Martini—very dry. No, order me two. I think I'm going to need some fortification."

"He said it was a hell of a swell idea. He said no one else would have thought of it. He said only new blood could come up with good creative suggestions like that."

"And so I'm to be punished for giving you a good idea, eh?"

"If it were only just *one* good idea . . . Two Martinis very dry, please."

"Don't try to blame it on that, Charlie. Whatever it is, it isn't *that*. You're the best brain-picker in the business, or I wouldn't have picked you to pick mine. You know damn well these kinds of ideas aren't any help to me, anyway, even if I *were* to suggest them instead of you; so why shouldn't you suggest them? I've got enough ideas in *my* line to keep Bruce aware of my worth, and these ideas are just random ones. So why shouldn't you suggest them? And you know it."

"In other words, you've got ideas to spare—enough for yourself and enough to go all the way around three times, and everyone'll be rich and successful and happy because you're a regular priceless idea factory. My hat's off to you, Marjorie."

"Happy birthday, Charlie," she said. "Don't ever change. Stay just as sweet as you are tonight. Promise?"

Before Charlie had taken the job at Cadence, he had not believed in the notion that stereotypes in life are unavoidable—nor that eventually, not only does one have to choose from stereotypes those who are to be his colleagues, lovers, friends, neighbors, and enemies, but also choose for himself his own stereotype.

Before Charlie had taken the job at Cadence, he had believed in the myth of unique individuality.

Perhaps he had believed in it because he had been too young to see its lie; too young to know that even "characters" were stereotypes of "characters" and that, ultimately, everyone could be classified. And perhaps he had believed in it because he had not, until he met Marge Mann, found himself in two such quite stereotype situations.

He was, in the one, the bright young man at the office having the affair with the more sophisticated and older and more important woman at the office.

He was, in the other, the married man who "inadvertently" had fallen into an affair with a woman, during the last month of his wife's pregnancy.

In both, Marge Mann was the woman—she, too, a stereotype: the woman-on-the-verge-of-forty, never married, attractive, aggressive, with an apartment where they could be alone, a good bar, a good bed, and the kind of lingerie and negligees most men appreciate.

What Charlie found unique in Marge were her inconsistencies.

She who could cuss like a fiction writer's version of a Marine sergeant, read Millay, Yeats, Swinburne, Keats —and read them with regularity too, Charlie knew—and was always reading them to him or quoting from them. She revived in him his own enthusiasm for poetry, which had been waning as he became more engrossed in the business world. She revived his interest in reading and, ultimately, in writing bits of poetry now and then —for Marge.

Joan had once—not long after Charlie met Marge— remarked about a Housman poem Charlie read to her one lazy Saturday afternoon when they were lolling about in the kitchen over coffee: "What do I think of it? . . . I think it's awfully gloomy. After all, life's not that bad, is it? . . . Go get the *Times,* darling, and see what's playing at Loew's."

Another of Marge's inconsistencies was that she was inconstant, and that from the very beginning she had not been an easy conquest, even when she was in love with Charlie. He was not yet in love with her but wanted her, enough to plead with her, though he had always felt it was disgusting to do so; and she had not been easy to take to bed.

Yet at Cadence, she had a reputation for being fast. There were even rumors that occasionally she cornered the boys down in the mailroom, and most all of them were under twenty.

The inconsistency of Marge's which Charlie enjoyed most of all, however, was her reluctance to let a quarrel begin between them. As hot-tempered and trigger-fingered as she was around the office, she always put Charlie off when he felt like arguing. And she very rarely started one herself.

And Charlie had never seen her cry except when she was terribly moved by something—a poem, a symphony, a gift, an orgasm.

Joan, in contrast, threw vases, slammed and locked doors, got migraine headaches, used up entire Kleenex boxes over one slight spat, and was not at all disinclined to fetch her suitcases from the attic and call the depot for train information.

In fact, up until that evening of March 6, 1939, Charlie and Marge had not really had a serious quarrel in the fifteen months they had been carrying on their affair.

Although it had begun at The Gotham, once again Marge had managed to abate it temporarily, by taking a package from her pocketbook just as the waiter brought their Martinis. This occurred just as Charlie had decided to tell Marge he wanted to call the whole thing off—not just because of Joan, not because it wasn't fair to Joan, but more because of Janie. He had Janie to think about. She was growing up and ga-ga-ing over telephones, and before long she'd be asking him why he wasn't coming home for dinner. And, finally she was his daughter; he had to be a decent father.

"What's this?" he said.

"Open it, darling . . . Remember that Millay poem I read you the other night."

"Hmm? Millay?"

"You know," and she recited as he fumbled with the wrapping:

This be our solace that it was not said
When we were young and warm and in our prime
We lay upon our couch as lie the dead
Sleeping away the unreturning time. . . .

"Remember?" she repeated. "I read it to you while we—"

"Keep it down!" Charlie said. "The people next to us have run out of conversation."

"I'm sorry, Charlie."

"I remember the poem," he said, taking the cover off the box. "I liked that poem. I remember it. I didn't mean to snap."

He took the gift out of the tissues.

"It's an hour glass," she said. "It's a keyholder for your car keys. You needed a new one."

Charlie fondled it appreciatively. "Thanks, Marge. Thanks, honey."

"It's supposed to sort of symbolize the unreturning time."

"It's swell," Charlie said.

"Do you really like it, darling?"

"I think it's swell, Marge," Charlie said, thinking now he'd *have* to stay with her at least until 9:30 or so. "Thanks," he said, suddenly wanting her, wanting her in a surprisingly desperate way, wanting to cling to her woman's body and feel the tears she gave him with love, there in the crease of his neck when she came against him. But in the months of their togetherness, Charlie had learned something. He couldn't just go home to bed with her and not feed her afterwards—that was crude. He couldn't do that to Marge, and tonight he hadn't the time, so he couldn't have her. And it was sad and maddening and frustrating, and he wasn't at all sure he didn't love her. In fact, he was very sure he did. And very sure he could blame Joan somehow for literally rushing him off his feet that summer and getting him married when he was too young for marriage. God, here he was just thirty-two and he had a wife and kid.

"Cheers!" Marge said.

Charlie clinked his glass against hers, aware that the people at the next table were now staring quite shamelessly, and had probably overheard the whole business between Marge and himself.

"Cheers!" Charlie said, thinking: what the hell, what the hell, what the hell:

> *as i caper and sing and leap*
> *i wake the world from sleep*
> *when i sing my wild free tune*
> *wotthehell wotthehell*

Where was that from anyway?
archy and mehitabel.

That's what Marge did for him—made him remember lines from poems he hadn't read since 1926. So he had a wife and kid; *wotthehell!*

But at dinner, over Oysters Rockefeller, Marge said: "Are you coming back with me afterwards, Charlie? For a little while?"

"I can't. I want to, but I can't."

"Oh . . . Well—if you *can't*—"

"Look, it's bad enough I'm coming home late on my birthday. She always plans things for me. I mean—special dishes."

"You're going to eat again?"

"Well, I didn't plan on eating all this. I was just going to have plain oysters."

"Oh, I see. Sort of progressive dinner, hmm?"

"Well what do you think? I mean, aren't you glad I'm able to spend this much time with you?"

"Yes, darling, I'm glad. I'd just be happier if you'd picked a night when you'd have more time."

"It's hard enough as it is. Now I'll have to eat two dinners tonight. One thing this affair will do for me is to make me fat as all get out."

"And the other, Charlie?"

"What other?"

"Or the *others?* The other *things* this affair will do for you?"

"Let's not spoil dinner, Marge."

"Well, you're going to have *two*, after all."

"Yes, that's right. On my goddam birthday I'm going to have dinner with my wife. Yes, that's right."

"All right, let's try to be calm. Let's change the subject, Charlie. Okay, tell me more about your talk with Bruce this noon."

"I told you. He liked *your* ideas. He may even give *me* a raise, they're so good."

"Charlie, do you realize that half those alleged ideas of mine are ideas you yourself think of when you're discussing business with me?"

"Come off it, Marge. We both know the score."

"I'm perfectly serious. The one about lowering the masthead, for instance. Remember that? We were sitting—"

"Does it make you feel better to think I *don't* pick your brains, Marge?"

"What do you mean by that?"

"I mean, then you don't have to think that all I want from this affair is a raise in pay and a promotion."

"Charlie!"

"Well, what are you trying to make me feel better for? Always trying to make me feel better! . . . Trying to make yourself feel better maybe!"

She put her fork down and stared at him. "Charlie, I was telling the truth. They aren't *all* my ideas. I wasn't trying to make you feel better, and I didn't feel bad at all—until you suggested a reason."

"It's what everybody thinks, isn't it?"

"What is?"

"That I'm hanging around you to get ahead."

"Suddenly I don't feel hungry."

"The day I walked into Cadence, you took me under your wing, didn't you? It was 'Charlie, watch out for this,' and 'Charlie, watch out for that.' And it was, 'Charlie, I think the better way of doing it would be this way,' and 'Charlie, one of Bruce's weaknesses is this,' and 'Charlie, Charlie, Charlie.' Wasn't it? . . How could I have missed!"

"It's funny," she said.

"What's funny? Tell me something funny."

"You have a guilty conscience."

"No kidding?"

"Don't be flip about this, Charlie. Please I never realized it . . . you actually doubt your own motivations, don't you? You actually think sometimes that the reason for us *is* a raise in pay and a promotion . . . I wonder why I never thought of that."

"Oh, eat your oysters, Marge. For the love of God, eat your oysters."

"I'm sorry. I'm just not hungry . . . In fact, I think I'd like to go home . . . alone."

"Don't make a scene," he said as she reached for her purse.

"I'm not going to. I'm just going home."

"Don't go home. That's silly. Eat your oysters and I'll drop you."

"No, I'm going. I really want to go."

"Marge, look, I'm all keyed up. I don't know—today when I called Joan to tell her I'd be late, she put Janie on the phone. It sort of annoyed me. I don't know. Let's keep our heads."

"Tonight wasn't my idea, Charlie. I knew she'd want you home."

"Eat your oysters," Charlie said. "I'm sorry."

"I'm going," she said, getting up.

"Don't be silly, please. Look, wait until I pay the check."

"Good-by, Charlie," she said.

She turned and started out the door.

Then Charlie suddenly realised something that surprised him, and he did a strange thing.

He knew all at once that he didn't love her—but at the same time he couldn't let her go.

He got up and ran after her, his napkin still tucked in his coat. Without paying the check, he ran out into the street where he found her hailing a cab.

He grabbed her arm. It had begun to rain, and both of them were getting wet. A cab pulled up for her; the door was open; but he held her arm to keep her from getting in.

"I love you, Marge," he said. "I love you. Don't go!"

"And I love you. But I want to go home alone."

"Why? Listen, I'll pay the check and come back and we'll go to your place together for a while. Listen, let's talk this out."

He wondered, even as he was pleading with her, why he couldn't let her go; why he didn't love her; why it was so necessary for her to wait for him, for him to convince her of the love he didn't feel.

"Will you wait?"

"No," she said. "And I'm getting wet."

The cab driver said, "You're getting the inside wet too, lady. Make up your mind."

"Good night, Charlie," she said.

She pulled her arm free, got in, and the cab went away. Charlie stood in the rain. People passing looked at him, at the napkin, at the cab vanishing down East Fifty-seventh.

Then Charlie walked back in, paid the check, and put his coat on.

For about ten minutes he walked in the rain, trying to think what it all meant, but he couldn't accept the idea that there really was anything at all mercenary in his relationship with Marge. And even if he wasn't *in* love with her, he loved her, didn't he? The way lots of men loved women who weren't their wives. Sure he did. He had wanted her so badly in the Gotham, he had felt it through to his loins—and he had tried not to have her, out of consideration for her, so was that mercenary? He loved her as a woman, as a person. It had nothing to do with anything else; not his job; not Joan or Jane; nothing or no one else.

At the corner of Sixtieth and Madison he realized he had left the gift, the key ring, back in the restaurant, and he thought of calling there and asking them to hold it for him. But when he hailed a cab to go home, he gave the address of the restaurant instead. He believed fully that that was further proof he really loved Marge Mann, as a person, as a woman . . . And he wished women wouldn't get so goddam serious all the time.

MARCH 6, 1957

CHAPTER EIGHT

WHEN Sandra Scott answered the telephone in her office, an instant reaction of annoyance came to her face, but she was careful to screen it from her voice before she replied, "Yes, Mr. Cadence will see Mr. Basescu."

Then, pressing the button to the intercom, she said, "Mr. Basescu is on his way up, Mr. Cadence."

"Basescu?"

"The writer, Mr. Cadence. The one who did the lead article for the *Vile* dummy . . . You remember, he had an appointment with Mr. Keene, but Mr. Keene had forgotten his doctor's appointment. You said you'd talk with him."

"What's the matter with Wally, always running to the doctor?"

"I think it's a head doctor, Mr. Cadence. Shall I send Mr. Basescu in when he arrives?"

"Yes, do that. And say, Sandy, any reaction from Charlie Gibson on the memo?"

"None to date, sir."

"You sound worried or something."

"No, Mr. Cadence. I'm not worried."

"I don't know . . . you sound different . . . Well, show him in when he gets there, won't you, Sandy?"

"I will," she said.

Sandra Scott had been his secretary for eight years. Their relationship was one of those peculiar secretary-boss ones in which he finds all he could ask for in a secretary, and she finds—a world.

Sandra Scott's mother knew the reason she was still unmarried at thirty-two was that she had compared every beau she had ever dated with Bruce Cadence—and found all of them wanting.

Her father wanted to know what was so special about Bruce Cadence, anyway. He had met Cadence—a man over sixty shorter than Sandra, fat, married happily, a father, and bald. So how could she even think of him as anything special?

"Since when has love had eyes?" Mrs. Scott would say.

And invariably, Sandra would take a long walk after such talk, up near Fort Tryon Park in Washington Heights where she lived; and she would wonder why they had to spoil it for her by insisting she was in love with Mr. Cadence. And she would promise herself for the 106th time that she would move out and get her own apartment. And invariably her broodings would end with the one thought: Why can't they understand that it's just a very deep feeling for a very fine person!

Sandra Scott was a large girl, a horsey girl—good-natured, efficient, gentle. And if love had no eyes, it did have ears, very sensitive ears, and it could hear everything that was being said about Bruce Cadence.

Once, she had even heard someone say something *he* had said about *her.*

"The reason I'm a successful business man and a happy family man," he had said, "is because I have a homely secretary."

That hurt more than anything had ever hurt.

But usually Sandra Scott heard criticism of Bruce Cadence—not because he was disliked by the majority, but simply because no one praised him behind his back.

She had grown accustomed to sifting out the distortions, and accepting the fact of his flaws. She had learned self-control in the face of both, but on the morning of March 6, 1957, Sandra Scott was hypersensitive to the office gossip.

Perhaps the most persistent criticism of Bruce Cadence was that he always needed a crutch, and that the crutch carried the bulk of the weight. They used to say Charlie Gibson was his crutch, that all of Bruce's editorial policies were Charlie's, that Bruce was incapable of doing anything on his own.

But Charlie Gibson, once he had put an end to his affair with Marge Mann, was well thought of by most everyone at Cadence and so there was nothing truly indignant in the criticism, and certainly little bitterness.

Wally Keene, on the other hand, was not well liked; nor were his ideas, which Bruce Cadence was currently in the process of putting into effect, popular.

Still, the employees at Cadence could forgive the idea of the *Vile* dummy, even if it was against their better judgment, for there was a chance that it would put Cadence Publications back on its feet.

Yet few of them would be able to forgive Wally Keene's decision about Marge Mann; and least of all, Sandra Scott.

To her it seemed shameful and incredible and fantastically cruel. When she thought about it, she remembered how she had somehow known the sort of operation Marge Mann was having performed, that week before Marge went to the hospital without telling them what was wrong. Sandra knew—and the knowledge had a strange effect upon her, for while she had always found Marge amusing and agreeable, she had never felt a kindred feeling for her until then. She had never felt truly concerned and upset about anyone at Cadence, other than Bruce Cadence, until then. And she never understood why; why *then?*

But it had depressed her to the point where she began to talk about it too much; until people noticed.

Her mother had said: "You'd think it was happening to you. Besides, this woman's almost sixty, isn't she? What difference does it make?"

Her father had said: "When are you going to stop worrying about other people and start worrying about yourself? I want to be a grandfather some day!"

Even Bruce Cadence noticed. "Sandy," he said, "you were never close to Marge, were you? How come all the interest?"

And she had answered: "I can't explain it. I just feel at a loss."

Then she had had the horrible nightmare about there being a mistake made, and instead of wheeling Marge into the operating room, *she* was being wheeled in. She was begging her mother to make them stop, while her mother said, "Well, you've only wasted your years anyway, being an office wife. What difference does it make?"

That morning Sandra thought about it all, and then about Mr. Basescu coming up to talk to Mr. Cadence. She remembered the last time she had seen Basescu— how she had felt an instantaneous revulsion at the thin little white-faced man with the narrow nicotine-stained fingers, the nails of which were tapered and too long; at the faint odor of stale liquor on his breath, the pearl stickpin in the seedy brown-and-yellow striped tie, at the voice, barely a whisper, at the way he seemed to hover over her as he spoke with her.

"You should be used to writers by now," Bruce Cadence had remarked upon her reaction. "They're a tacky lot. I think you're just bothered because of the article he wrote."

When the door opened and Basescu entered, Sandra felt that revulsion a second time. She barely spoke to him. Then, quickly, she went to open Mr. Cadence's door.

Bruce Cadence rose to meet Elliot Basescu, and pointed to a deep brown leather chair beside his desk.

"I'm sorry about the mix-up in Wally's appointments," he said, "but I know what he wanted to talk with you about. As a matter of fact, I called it to his attention."

Basescu fumbled for a cigarette, lit it, and leaned forward, clutching it between his fingers. "I didn't get my check," he said.

"That's routine. It'll go through on the third Wednesday of the month."

"I was afraid you had found something wrong with the article."

"Not really wrong, but there's one thing in it that I'm a little wary about."

Cadence paced as he talked, his arms behind his back: "That episode at college, the one in which he paid a fraternity brother to let him—" Cadence fumbled for words "—to let him, well, you remember that, eh?"

"Yes. Quite vividly."

"The point is, all through the article the information has been handled more as a hint than as a fact we state conclusively. I mean, we've used words like 'alleged' often, and 'said to be.' That can make all the difference in a courtroom on this type of story."

"He won't take it to court, believe me."

"But, Elliot, it isn't our business to concern ourselves with whether or not a subject will take us to court. We just have to be darn certain that, should we find ourselves there, we'll come out the winners."

"All right . . . what's the problem?"

"Now, in every instance we've been able to verify the facts we have presented, but in the college incident we can't even come close to verifying it. And remember, it involves a specific fraternity."

"That can be deleted."

"Right, but I think the whole incident should be deleted."

"Then," Basescu said, "we aren't as well documented. Besides, it kills a lot of the suspense."

"But we don't even know the name of the boy he did this to."

"Don't we?"

"Well, I don't," Cadence said. "Where'd you dig the fact up, anyway?"

Basescu smiled at his cigarette in a preoccupied way.

"Well, you don't have to tell me, because I'm quite sure I'm going to delete it."

"I think it'll ruin the story," Basescu said.

"When are you due back in St. Louis?"

"A few days."

"Then you'll have time to rewrite?"

"Are you going to insist?"

"I think so, Elliot."

"It's a mistake." Basescu ground out his cigarette as though he were squashing a bug. "It's a mistake."

"Elliot, sometimes I think you have a personal gripe against him."

"The dinner hour will be quieter all over America."

"Yes," Cadence said, "but I'm afraid I don't get very much of a kick when I think about it. That's the dirty side to this. A man's bread snatched out from under him because we need to sell magazines."

"Maybe he won't be fired because of it."

"Oh, Elliot, face up. The man is sponsored by a soap company and soap is used in the home. It's associated with cleanliness. And, after all, Otto Avery is always associated with current events. Nobody wants a sodomist reading off the news from the Pope or Princess

Margaret or the cold-war fronts, much less at the dinner hour."

"He really isn't a very pleasant person. If you knew how unpleasant he was, you wouldn't think twice."

"You knew him well, hmm?"

"Yes," Basescu said, "and I knew the boy in the fraternity house quite well too. He was a nice boy; a serious student, a rather shy boy, not as worldly as Avery. Avery corrupted him. Literally corrupted him, ruined his life. If it weren't for Avery, he might have been a very great scholar, or a literary figure of some sort."

Cadence shook his head thoughtfully. "I don't know. It's my own opinion that nobody corrupts someone else, not that way. And the boy did take money."

"He was very poor," Basescu said. "His family struggled to put him through college."

"Well, we're going to delete that section, Elliot. Just take it and delete it, and try to fill in with some of the minor facts we struck out on the earlier version."

Basescu shrugged and lit another cigarette, sucking the smoke into his lungs, meditating. Bruce Cadence couldn't avoid staring at the man's filthy fingernails, at the general unwashed look of him.

Basescu said, "There's something else."

"Yes?"

"This Gibson. Has he read this yet?"

"Charlie? He'll read it today."

"You see, he knew Avery too. He hated him as much as—" Basescu paused and looked at his cigarette. "He went to college with him, too. He didn't like him any more than anyone did, but still—"

"Did you know Charlie, Elliot?"

"I knew him. Very vaguely . . . I'd rather he didn't know that I wrote this piece. Wally assured me there'd be no reason for him to know."

"You're using a pseudonym."

"That's correct. I just want to be sure. Just in case

there should be any—well, reaction on the part of Gibson."

"Yes," Cadence said thoughtfuly, "there may well be . . . This sort of thing doesn't set well with Charlie. I didn't know he knew Avery personally."

"He hated him. Avery pulled a rather disagreeable trick on him at one time. Surprised him with a young lady, *flagrante delicto.*"

"You all knew each other fairly well, hmm?"

Basescu said, "Not truly. But a story like that circulates on a campus."

"Would Charlie know about Avery paying this boy?"

"I doubt it," Basescu said. "Very few people knew about it."

Bruce Cadence rose and stood by his desk, in the perfunctory gesture of the executive calling the interview to a close.

There was something about Elliot Basescu that made Cadence uncomfortable; uncomfortable in the same way one is when eating a sandwich at a soda fountain manned by an acne-faced fellow in a soiled white apron. Yet there was more to it than simply the revulsion at the physical appearance of Basescu; there was a feeling about him, an aversion much like the one Sandy had suggested to Bruce Cadence when she had first encountered the man. Cadence felt it throughout their interview, and in some remote fashion he felt that he was allied with the man—and not simply in this despicable scheme to expose the newscaster; having entered into that business alliance, he was automatically an ally of Basescu's in all ways. He experienced an uncanny wave of self-disgust, one which came upon him so suddenly that his voice snapped as he said, "That'll be all, Elliot."

Basescu noticed the tone. He raised an eyebrow, regarding Cadence momentarily, as though he understood. Then, tamping out his cigarette, he stood up.

He said, "Have you decided on a name for the magazine yet?"

"We call it *Vile* in dummy form," Cadence answered.

A grim smile moved Basescu's lips. "Very amusing," he said, "and so it is. But it would be even more vile to go hungry, don't you think? Of course, money isn't everything. But then, who wants everything?"

He stood picking at his fingernails for a slow second.

Then he spoke again: "And it is even more vile," he said, "to imagine that the fear of poverty could be so overwhelming in the mind of a young boy, that he would accept a degenerate's immoral proposition. And by accepting it—" he snapped his short, knobby fingers— "ruin his life."

Bruce Cadence looked squarely at Basescu, uncertain of the insight Basescu's words had lent him suddenly. But sure in his tone, he said: "I don't think I feel sorry for that boy."

"Oh?"

"Anyway," and Cadence was curt, "I want it out of the story."

"The fact still remains," Elliot Basescu answered, turning to go, "but it's your magazine." He made a mock salute to his forehead with his finger. "So anything you say. Good day."

"Good-by."

Cadence stood woodenly for a moment. Then, impulsively, he flicked back the button of his intercom. His voice was angry, and his hands knotted the rubber cord as he spoke. "Haven't we got any kind of reaction at all from Gibson on that memo yet, Sandy?" he said.

"No, Mr. Cadence."

"Well, what the hell is this! What's Charlie doing down there?"

"Shall I call him for you, sir?"

"Yes," Bruce Cadence said. "Yes!" Then, "No . . . no . . . never mind. No, Sandy. See if Wally's back from the doctor, will you?"

"Anything you say," Sandra Scott replied.

It sounded just the way Elliot Basescu had said it. ". . . so anything you say. Good day."

CHAPTER NINE

A⁣T TEN minutes to twelve, Charlie Gibson sat at his desk, holding the memo he had just read: ". . . that in view of these facts, it is necessary for Cadence Publications to take definite action with regard to Miss Mann." The words kept running through his mind—the words and a host of flash memories, helter-skelter ones, the burnt-out end of bygone days that spanned what seemed like years and years:

1942—At the Oak Room, in the Plaza, drinking stingers.

"Wasn't it awful about the fire, papa-doodle?" she said. "Who'd ever thought The Cocoanut Grove would just—phfft—burn down like that. Huh? . . . Papa-doodle?"

"Don't have any more to drink, Marge."

"I know, papa-doodle, it's a very solemn time. The Nazis are riding up and down in Eiffel Tower, and little ole Charlie's gonna go over there an' make 'em stop, huh?"

"I tried to tell her. What could I tell her? Could I say, 'Look, I'm going to war, but I'm not coming back to you or Janie. There's somebody else.' Could I say that?"

"Mercy, no, papa-doodle! Hunt-uh! You just go off and get those Nazis off that tower, 'n, then come back and tell her. After she waited for you."

"Marge, I love you. I love *you*. I don't love Joan. I never realized how much I love you until the morn-

81

ing my orders came through. I knew, but I didn't know how much. I just sat at my desk thinking: I can't leave Marge. My God, I can't leave her. That's honestly what I thought . . . Not Joan. I thought, I can't leave Marge."

"Or little sweet dimple-kneed Janie, huh, papa-doodle?"

"I love Janie."

"Me and Janie oughtta have a club. A lots-a-luck club."

"But I can't just tell Joan now. Don't you see? What good would it do?"

"We could have our week up in Vermont, papa-doodle."

"We can have that anyway. I'll see to it."

"Thanks, papa-doodle. That's all it'll take. A big ole week in Vermont, and little Margie will wait and wait and wait and wait for Charlie to come back from that tower. I want another stinger."

"Please, don't have another."

"Order Joan around, not me, papa-doodle. I'm strictly a free-lancer, you know."

"I love you, Marge. I mean it about asking Joan for the divorce. When I come home, I swear I will."

"When Charlie comes marching home again . . . Hurrah, hurrah! I'll have a stinger while I'm waiting, papa-doodle."

1939—At the entrance to The Southgate Apartments.

". . . and I want you to believe one thing, Charlie: I think you're doing the right thing. With all my heart, I believe that."

"I knew you'd take it this way. God you're a good person, Marge. You've done so much for me. I hate to end it like this but—"

"Charlie, let's get one thing straight. I didn't do anything for you. Not a thing. You used to think you got your ideas from me, remember? Well, you know better now. They weren't mine. You're quick, and you're bright, and you're young. I used to sit across from you in a restaurant when we were talking shop, and I'd see those wheels turning. I was *with* you, yes. But it was Charlie Gibson doing the brain work. You know that, don't you?"

"I guess so," Charlie said.

"You're one hell of a guy, Charlie. We've had a fabulous time. I think I want to leave it at that. Okay?"

"Okay," Charlie said.

" 'By now."

Charlie said, "Good-by, Marge."

1944

Dear Charlie,

I'm a little confused, papa-doodle. I thought it was G.I. Joe who was supposed to get the "Dear John" routine. Never occurred to me it was G. D. Marge . . . So it's 'just one of those things' now, hmmm? And when Captain Gibson takes to mufti again, Marge goes on the shelf.

Glad to hear war's made you "think things through realistically," as you put it, my darling. Wonder if in this wave of realism it ever occurred to you that brain-pickers, when they start trying to figure things out for themselves, have the same luck cripples do minus the crutches. Not that you're a brain-picker, papa-doodle, but how come you just fell flat on your face?

Good luck learning to walk. Hope you can stay in step at Cadence upon your return. If you need help, doubtless you'll think of,

Your Margie.

1942—In the Eagle Room, at The Montpelier Tavern, Vermont.

"Charlie, do you feel like finishing dinner?"

"No."

"Let's not."

"I love you."

"I love being Mrs. Charles Johnston. You know, Charlie, I'll settle for this. For this week. I don't want anything more—except for you to come home safely."

"I love you, Marge."

"Pay the check, Mr. Johnston. I'll get the room key."

1945—Waiting for the elevator in the lobby of the Cadence Building.

"Bless my soul! Charlie!"

"Hi, Marge."

"Charlie! Well, welcome home, mister."

"Thanks."

"I guess I can call you mister now, hmm?"

"That's right."

"All ready to go back to the grind?"

"You bet!"

"Good to have you back."

"Good to be back."

"See you."

"Righto."

1940—12th floor, Apartment 1201, Southgate Apartments.

"I'm going to tell Joan tomorrow."

"You mean you're going to ask her, darling. You don't tell a wife you want a divorce, you ask her."

"Turn toward me a minute."

"That better?"

"That's wonderful. Ummmm."

1946—Over lunch, at the Algonquin.

"I'm glad we're friends, Charlie. I'm glad it all worked out this way."

"I am, too."

"It could have been messy. Very messy. But the way it was, Joan never knew. And we knew the best of each other."

"And the worst, I guess. Or at least *you* knew the worst."

"I can't remember anything about us but the good things, Charlie. I try to remember the bad times, but I can't. I can only remember that we were always laughing."

"You're right. We had a lot of laughs."

"Here's mud in your eye."

"Health, Charlie. Health, wealth, and happiness."

1956—Outside the Cadence Building.

"I hear you're going to the hospital."

"That's right, Charlie. Tomorrow."

"It's nothing serious?"

"Not much more than a check-up. Besides, you know my resilient nature. Always bounce back."

"Good luck."

"Thanks. See you."

1943—From San Francisco.

Dear Marge, I've decided to ask Joan for a divorce. Darling, as soon as you get this letter, put in a call to me. It's important that you call *before* the

23rd, which should give you ample time. I want you
to agree with everything I am going to say in this
letter, before I write Joan; and I want to explain
it to you fully.

I can't go on any longer without you. I want to
marry you. It isn't fair to deceive Joan any longer.
I'll be shipping out most any day after the above
date. Joan can arrange for the divorce, and that
will mean I must give up custody of Janie. That's
going to *hurt*. But when I come home, you and I,
Marge will . . .

1943—From San Francisco.

MISS MARGE MANN
SOUTHGATE APARTMENTS
NEW YORK, NEW YORK
IGNORE LETTER STOP CONFUSED STOP WILL
WRITE IN DETAIL LOVE CHARLIE.

1943—From New York.

CAPTAIN CHARLES GIBSON
APO (7) 96
SAN FRANCISCO, CALIFORNIA
WHAT LETTER STOP LOVE MARGE

1943—Top-of-The-Mark, San Francisco

"I'm telling you, Dave, that's the way she took it.
Just pretended she never even got it. She's one hell of
a mature woman."

"Maybe she didn't get it, Charlie."

"No, she got it. It was over a week after I sent the letter when I wired her. I just knew I couldn't dissolve my marriage with Joan. I just walked in and sent the wire."

"She's a sport."

"I'll say, Dave. I'm not even going to mention the matter when I write her in the future. I think somehow time will find the right thing for all of us, me and Joan and Marge."

"Drink up, Captain, and get the waiter's eye."

1956—By the elevators in the Cadence Building, after lunch.

"Hi, papa-doodle. Goin' up?"

"Oh-oh, how many've you had?"

"A good many, papa-doodle. Don't you know I'm a lush lately. Of late, papa-doodle."

"How about a walk around the block, Marge. Seriously."

"Hell with it, papa-doodle. I'm strictly free-lance, remember? So hell with it. Leggo my arm."

March 6, 1957

MEMO FROM BRUCE CADENCE

To: Charlie Gibson
    cc: Wally Keene

It has been called to my attention that the Editor of our shelter magazine has been a source of conspicuous public embarrassment to Cadence Publications by appearing in an inebriated condition at numerous functions which she attended as our official representative.

In addition, I have received reports that she has been drinking in her office from time to time; and that more often she does not report to work until *after* lunch, and then, not infrequently, she appears in a state of near intoxication.

Furthermore, I have been greatly displeased with the quality of YOUR HOME in the past year. We have lagged way behind the other shelter books.

For example:

YOUR HOME was the very last to indulge the new consumer's craze, "do-it-yourself"; and then, for its initial article along these lines chose a "do-it-yourself" den—specifically, for the man of the house. Since our product is directed at the *young* homemaker, the den idea seems inconsistent. Young homemakers, newlyweds and the like, if they have any surplus rooms in their ranch house, bungalow, or apartment (I felt that the designation "ranch house" was over-reaching our consumer) would undoubtedly be more interested in a nursery or playroom. Dens are for middle-aged consumers, or consumers out of the "watch-the-budget" class. A sad beginning for "do-it-yourself" in YOUR HOME, I felt.

Also, there has been too much stress on the creative aspects of homemaking and less stress on the *practical*. The *young* homemaker wants to know how, and *needs* to know how, before she can innovate on her own.

In addition, the recipes have featured food far above our consumers' price range. Venison and the like are not *young* homemakers' daily fare, and we cater to their needs, not their extravagances.

It is apparent to me that in view of these facts, it is necessary for Cadence Publications to take definite action with regard to Miss Mann.

Were it not for the fact of her persistent insobriety, I would advise that she be assisted by a younger editor who would better identify with the young homemaker; and that she take a cut in pay.

In the past, her record at Cadence was excellent, and ordinarily I would feel that this fact warranted loyalty on our part.

However, there can be no leniency with an employee who has taken to liquor, and certainly not with a woman who would represent us in the shelter field in *any* capacity.

Therefore I am directing you to request Miss Mann's resignation, effective this day, March 6, 1957; two weeks' pay.

Bruce Cadence, President.

Charlie Gibson slapped the memo on the desk, and hit it hard once, with his fist. He saw that it was nearly noon, and he leaned on his elbows, thinking how he hated Keene's guts; hated the gross exaggeration of the memo, the flimsy evidence offered with respect to the decline in quality of *Your Home*, the insidious suggestion that Marge was an alcoholic, far beyond repair. Christ, she *always* drank . . . And that mincing "two weeks' pay" squeaked out at the end of the memo.

For a second or two he entertained the idea of charging up to Cadence's office and blowing his top, of going at Bruce the way he used to, head-on in hot rage, saying what he thought straight out. He wanted to say that he was fed up to here with young Keene's step-on-the-toes, go-for-the-buck business philosophy, that all of Keene's ideas were as vile as the dummy, and that if Marge Mann went, Charlie went—that as a matter of fact, Charlie should have gone the day Keene came.

He would like to have done just that, and he wondered why he didn't, why he just sat and let the anger boil through him.

He didn't know why.

In a sweeping glance at his desk he saw the letter from his daughter; the memo; and the untouched dummy for *Vile;* and he thought how rotten everything was suddenly, how really rotten everything was.

Then a dozen noon whistles blew.

MARCH 6, 1957

CHAPTER TEN

AT NOON, Joan Gibson double-checked the arrangements for the party that evening.

It was going to be a surprise for Charlie.

She had invited the Tullets and the Carrolls, their very best friends; and Anna was going to cook chicken tetrazzini, Charlie's favorite dish.

After she had finished going over the list with Anna, in the kitchen, she got up from the table and stood facing the window, looking out at the snow-splotched lawn, trying to think if there were anything she had forgotten.

She was ten years younger than Charlie, and she looked ten years younger than she was—a thin, slender woman with black hair cut in the short-cropped Italian style, and a good, soft profile. She had large, dark flashing eyes, and a mouth with lips she thought were too small. As a type she was tweeds, tapered slacks, skirts and sweaters, station wagons and shaggy-looking poodles—but with a flair, always; a very feminine flair.

She belonged in Greenwich. And in the summers when Charlie and she roughed it out at their cottage in Fair Harbor, on Fire Island, she belonged there.

Those years during which she and Charlie lived on Central Park West were the only ones she had ever spent as a city-dweller; and she had hated it.

But a lot of times she thought the reason she had such disagreeable feelings about city-living, when she thought back on it, was that when she and Charlie had that apartment, he had been involved with another woman. And Joan Gibson had never suspected it until Charlie made that awful mistake when he was in San Francisco—the mistake of writing Marge Mann a letter of proposal, then absent-mindedly addressing it to his wife.

Even now—after all the years since that morning when she had opened the envelope and begun to read: "Dear Marge, I've decided to ask Joan for a divorce—" she could never quite forget the feeling of utter despair that had overwhelmed her, the sense of mute bereavement that was a shadow cast across the days that followed when she didn't know what to do about it —whether to call him and tell him, whether to write him, whether to simply readdress the letter to the person Charlie had intended it for, whether to pack her and Janie's things and go home to Auburn, New York . . .

"Don't do a damn thing," Aileen Tullet had advised, "not a damn thing! Just pretend you never got it, and wait and see. This is war, honey. Everything's confused."

"I can't believe Charlie loves another woman, Aileen. I simply can't believe it."

"Have you heard it from the horse's mouth?"

"I've *read* it. Over and over."

"But he hasn't told you, honey. At least he doesn't think he has. Take my advice—until he does tell you, just sit tight. Don't mention the letter—ever; and don't do a damn thing about it."

Joan Gibson never did.

Less than a week after Charlie had mailed it, he called her to say he was shipping out. He also told her he loved her, that he wanted her, that he wished to hell the goddam war was over and he was back with his "two girls."

"Meaning me and Janie?" she had said.

Charlie said, "Who else?"

And maybe because Joan Gibson was perfectly

sincere when she had told Aileen Tullet that she simply could not accept the thought of Charlie's loving another woman, she never had to.

More than once, and from the very beginning, Joan's persistent incredulity had been an asset, from the time she sat on the yacht club dock up in Auburn, New York, listening to Charlie tell her of his love for Mitzie Thompson (thinking only, This is the man I'm going to marry)—to the time Charlie held her in his arms on a night they had accomplished simultaneous climaxes for the first time in their marriage, and he had told her very solemnly that he didn't want children—ever (completely oblivious to the fact she had, as usual, done nothing to prevent their conception, for the very reason she did want them).

When Charlie came home from Missouri University the summer he was graduated, and took Joan out on "a friendly date," he said—toward the end of the evening as he was fumbling under her sweater to rehook her bra—"My God, Joan, what's happening to us? We're supposed to be buddies. What's happening?"

"I don't know," she whispered in a shy tone. But she did know; she knew perfectly well what was happening to them, and she thought to herself that it was about time.

And the evening that she announced to Charlie that he was going to be a father in exactly seven months, the year they were living in the cold-water flat down on Bleecker Street in the Village, she knew then too —perfectly well—that Charlie would rave, "Well, you've got to get rid of it! Look, we can't afford it! I don't want children!" and that ultimately he would be helping her up and down steps, worrying over the fact she never had any strange desires for pickles in the middle of the night, pacing the hospital corridors importantly, fearfully, anxiously—and eventually referring to their progeny as "*my* Janie."

That noon, Joan Gibson turned from the window in the kitchen to face the maid. "Anna, is there anything you can think of that we've forgotten?"

"No, ma'am. Unless you're serious about wrapping up Mr. Gibson's old re-soled shoes."

"That's right! The shoes."

"I don't know what kind of a birthday gift that is," Anna muttered.

"Mr. Gibson will know," Joan Gibson said.

At noon, Bruce Cadence paused by Sandra Scott's desk on his way out to lunch.

"Nothing from Charlie's office yet, hmmm?"

"No. Nothing."

Cadence sat on the edge of the mahogany desk, his hat in his lap, his tweed topcoat over his arm. He frowned thoughtfully, rubbing his pudgy chin with his short, square fingers. "Charlie's changed, hasn't he?"

"A great deal has changed, Mr. Cadence."

"Remember the old Charlie? He used to come up and give me hell about all sorts of things. He was usually right too. I needed him, depended on him. I don't know. Maybe he just grew older."

"And if he were to give you hell about firing Marge Mann, would he be right?"

"No, Sandy. He'd be wrong."

"I wonder."

"That bothers you, doesn't it? It wasn't an easy thing for me to do—make that decision . . . No, it isn't that. It's the whole business. He hasn't even commented on the exposé magazine lately. Oh, I know he doesn't like the idea, but he hasn't really been adamant."

"Maybe he didn't have the chance, Mr. Cadence. Around Mr. Keene."

"That never used to stop Charlie. He could always shout it out. He always did. He was never a memo-sender. Didn't used to be."

"Before Keene, he wasn't. But B.K., a lot of things were different."

"Sandy, as a personality, Keene may not be very

agreeable, but as a troubleshooter, he's a good man.
He's got confidence; he's sure, and he's thorough!"

Sandra Scott said drily, "Oh, he's all of those. No
one's denying that."

"What do you mean the same thing used to happen
with your mother?" the doctor asked, glancing at his
watch, noting it was noon, getting hungry, thinking,
Only fifteen minutes more with this analysand; feel
like a potato salad for lunch; feel just like one but got
to watch the waistline.

"She destroyed my confidence too. I was never sure
around her either. It always turned out she was right.
Well, it's the same way with Marge Mann. When I
suggested the den idea for the do-it-yourself feature,
she said it wouldn't go over. She said the same thing
Bruce said—that it over-reached our advertisers' consumer . . . But I insisted on it, anyway . . . That and
the venison recipes . . . They were my ideas, and they
were bad ones. I couldn't admit they were mine."

The young man squirmed on the couch where he
lay and hit a side of it with his fist. "Damn!" he said,
"I'm going crazy! Why should I feel guilty? She's a
drunk, an awful drunk. Last week at a party Continental Electric threw for homemaking editors she
got up in the middle of everyone's eating and began
to sing some song. 'Frigging in the Rigging' or something like that. She's a drunk!"

The doctor decided he would settle for bacon and
tomato on toast.

"But I'm right to fire her, aren't I?" the young man
asked. "Should I be so goddam insecure because I
suggested it? She's a drunk!"

"What do you think?" the doctor said.

"If people at Cadence ever knew I was lying here
saying these things they'd— Yes, I'm right to fire her.
I think the reason I'm so worked up over it is that I'm
confusing Marge and my mother. That's all. That's
why I've lost sleep and been so goddam nervous. I

hated my mother so! She was one of those C-cup
bitches too."

"What exactly *is* a C-cup bitch?" the doctor asked.
The young man began. "She's the worst kind of bitch
there is. She's as power-happy as she is top-heavy. Our
business is brimming over with them—ours and—"

Yes, the doctor thought, bacon and tomato on toast,
with lettuce and mayonnaise.

At noon, Marge Mann thought of something which
had happened a couple of weeks ago. Psychologists call
it displacement, what she was doing—stopping in the
aura of a larger misery to dwell on a lesser one, and
worry it with the same force; but the scene came to
mind as she sat at her desk at noon, remembering a
midnight she had taken a cab after Blance Phelan's
housewarming party in the Village.

It had been a rotten evening—a 'hen party' populated
by food editors like herself; yet not. They dotted the
living room with their plump legs crossed beneath
their "basic" dresses, their countenances bovine and
delighted. Giggling, they reached for the ginger punch
passed on a tray with "ahs" and "ohs" and "Blance,
darling, did you use a Chablis in this, or is it a white
burgundy?" And a few of them hummed along to the
bland waltzes emanating from the hi-fi.

While Marge stood restlessly by the fireplace, fingering a shell Blance had found one summer on Shelter
Island, thinking to herself: f'chrissake *ginger punch—*
and later, back in the kitchen, gratefully accepted the
shot of James Pepper Blance offered her in a tumbler,
trying to sound casual before Blance's concerned eyes,
trying to keep her tone steady as she said, "Thanks. By
God, I will have a little, Blance. You're sweet!"

The others—after Swiss Fondue served "cafeteria
style"—played bridge and Scrabble and spoke of a jelly
sauce for fritters; showed photographs of Jerry "two
years old now" and Angie "taken at the picnic at Riis
Park." They admired Blance's tambour desk in the

foyer, and spoke of best-sellers; talked toward the end
of the evening of leaving "soon"; laughed and sighed
for long seconds afterward, smiling and smoothing
their skirts to their thighs with capable and contented
fingers, glad and enjoying themselves.

While Marge barely touched the food on her plate,
thought of excuses to make trips back and forth from
the kitchen, watering down the bourbon near the end
of the evening so Blance wouldn't notice how much
was gone from the bottle. She felt headaches come and
go, and worried when her hands shook while lighting
a cigarette and two of the guests noticed and looked
quickly away, nudging one another, shocked. And
Marge wondered if she had ever really cared, ever in
that long ago, about Fricasseed Giblets or Hot Ham
Mousse Supreme or Baked Quinces? As they *still* cared,
had she *ever?* Must have!

The others, when it was over, took cabs, doubled up,
intending to drop one another en route. They sang
good-bys happily at Sheridan Square, some going uptown, some down or cross.

While Marge feigned an appointment "just down the
street," too tight to care how improbable it sounded
—this appointment at midnight—and walked, none too
steadily, into a drugstore, into a phone booth, to wait
out their going. And she sat momentarily, desperate
for a drink. Then she remembered the wadded Kleenex
in her handbag, and its contents saved since lunch.
She reached in and unfolded the tissue, took out the
lemon peel which she had taken from the Martini,
touched it to her lips, and from it sucked the memory
of the taste of gin, sucked it with a savage satisfaction,
until it was safe to leave, and get a drink in the bar
at the corner.

She had two.

She slugged them down, one after the other. Most
everyone in the bar was watching Steve Allen's show,
but one man was watching her.

He said, "Thirsty, baby?"

She hated Greenwich Village because of men like that.

He said, "Hey, Lillian Roth, sing us something!"

She tossed down two dollars, eager for her change, but again he said, "Hey, Lillian Roth, sing us something!"

Hurrying, she lurched to the door and out into the street.

The cab was waiting on the corner.

"Eventually," she told the driver, finding considerable difficulty with the word, "I want to go to Southgate 'partments. Know where they are?"

"Sure," he said.

"Sure," she said. "But first I want to go to a nightcap. Not down in this damn stinking hole. Filled with all kinds 'generates. Good for nothings!"

"Greenwich Village," the driver smirked, "where the boys wear their hair long and the girls wear their hair short." He laughed enthusiastically at his own joke. Then, "Where to?"

"Upto'n someplace," she said. "Don't have to drink in this stinking hole, huh?"

"No, ma'am," he said.

She said, "Someplace uptown . . . What's your name?"

"Roosevelt," he said.

"I voted for you," she said. "Now get me a nice something that looks and tastes like bourbon, papa-doodle."

"Sure," he said, looking at her through his mirror. "Okay."

For a while they rode in silence. He kept watching her. She had something in her hand. She was holding it to her mouth, sucking on it. A lemon peel.

He said, "I got a little something that could tide you over."

"You *have*, papa-doodle?"

"Yeah," he said. "Gotta be careful though. Can't just pass it to you on the main drag."

"Look," she said, "go where you can, huh? Mamma-doodle's not quite up to par, papa-doodle."

He chuckled. "Okay, mamma-doodle."

He went crosstown, way East, passing warehouses. She sat behind him, scratching matches in an effort to light a cigarette. She couldn't light it, and she cursed.

He said, "In a minute now."

She said, "Where the hell are we, papa-doodle?"

"It's all right," he said. "Here, it's all right."

He pulled the cab up to the curb behind a big truck, cut his lights, and waited momentarily, looking around him.

"Where's the drink, papa-doodle?"

"Coming up," he said.

He leaned down and unwrapped a leather jacket, pulling out a bottle. Uncapping it, he passed it back to her.

"Sorry, no glass."

She didn't answer. She lifted the bottle and drank. Some of the whisky spilled down her chin. She wiped it with the back of her hand and licked her hand. She sighed.

"Good?" he said.

"Very good, papa-doodle. I'm glad I voted for you."

Again, he looked around him; then he said, "Want me to light your cigarette?"

"I'd like a cigarette," she said. "I'm out of matches. Used them all damn up."

He said, "I'll help you." He opened his door, testing her reaction.

"Okay?" he asked.

"You're nice, papa-doodle," she answered.

While he got out of the front seat and moved into the back seat he saw her drink again from the bottle, a long drink.

She smoked the cigarette he lit for her, one or two drags—then its ash grew long as it rested between her fingers on her lap, and she drank more while he watched her.

When the cigarette fell from her fingers onto her coat, he pushed it to the floor and squashed it with his foot, then placed his hand back on her coat, over her thigh.

He said, "Bet you got on a pretty dress, nice lady like you."

"You're nice, papa-doodle," she said. "What time you got to be home, papa-doodle?"

"No time," he said, opening her coat.

"You going to stay the night?" she said. "Huh, papa-doodle?"

"Sure," he said. "Sure, mamma-doodle."

Gently he pushed her back down on the seat.

She was docile as he prepared her; out cold as he relieved himself.

But the next morning, when miraculously she had awakened in her hide-a-bed and tried to remember getting there from the Village, she remembered suddenly the name "Roosevelt"; then for some slow minutes nothing more than the name; until from the depths of her memory came the black hands working on her clothes, the feeling of cold leather on her bare skin; and a long while after an angry voice commanding her to "Put them on now, damn it! You got to look right when I drop you! Or you'll get out now. I'll leave you here!"

She remembered being scared of his voice, wondering who he was, wanting desperately to get awake enough to obey him, fearing desertion, wanting to work her fingers and dress herself—and somehow being able to.

She remembered sitting up in the seat because he snapped: "Sit up, damn it! You got to sit up. Act like a fare!"

She remembered whimpering as he drove, wondering why he was mean.

The next morning, she remembered and suddenly she knew what she had done, knew the nadir she had reached. And while she poured a drink, standing naked in her kitchenette, staring out at the cold, impersonal stone towers of Manhattan, she couldn't even cry, or jump from the ledge she stood before, or pray, or ask for help from anyone. Who, anyway? She could do nothing but reach behind her for a refill.

At noon, Marge Mann remembered, then stopped remembering that, and dug down into her bucket bag for the flask.

The door of her office was closed, but she drank from the flask in a quick, furtive way; drank deeply. God, it felt good. By now she knew she was through at Cadence, and wondered what induced that homely secretary of Bruce Cadence's to sneak down and warn her. Always thought she looked like a Polish maid on Sunday, the way she dressed in those ugly satin blouses and frizzed her hair; God, the bourbon went down fine. Well, what was she going to *do*, for the love of dear Christ. Canned at sixty. Hand in your resignation. What the hell was that ugly Scott bag misty-eyed about? What the hell was going on? Hands are shaking. Charlie will notice at lunch hands are shaking. Play it cool at lunch; never let him know how it feels on the ash-heap; not Charlie. Loved him once. How'd everything get so old so quick? Just going to sit there at lunch and play it down; won't even take a drink; show Charlie they're wrong; get the whizz down now and won't even take a drink; got mints in my change purse; clear my breath. God, what *now?* Scared, God, scared; shaking—shaking—

Dear Janie. Charlie composed the letter in his mind as he put on his overcoat and headed for lunch. *I've never refused you anything, have I? But it hurts me to have you ask for money to—*
  Dear Janie, if you try to carry out your plans for going to Europe with that shiftless Harvard boy, I'm going to write your dean and—

*Janie dearest, I'm catching the next train to Rad-
cliffe and—*
   Dean of Women
   Radcliffe College
   Cambridge, Mass.
   Madam:
   *It has been called to my attention that my daugh-
ter—*
   "Happy birthday, Mr. Gibson," someone shouted as
he neared the elevators.
   Charlie saw Bonnie, and the girl with her who was
beaming at him. He said to the girl, "Thank you."
   *Dearest Janie, I love you so. Don't hurt yourself this
way—*
   Then someone was tugging at his sleeve, pulling him
aside in a confidential way. Looking down, he saw
Bonnie.
   "Well?" she said.
   "Well what?"
   "Well, the memo? Marge Mann."
   "I have to fire her," Charlie said.
   Bonnie murmured, "Dear God!"
   Dear Janie, Charlie thought; while the mind's ver-
satility summoned up some bygone memory of a hide-
a-bed, a bourbon, and the sensual smell of a woman
after love; then flung an accusation at him: Janie never
had a chance. You were having an affair when she was
growing up. Needed her father—any psychologist would
tell you; followed by miscellaneous remembered sent-
ences: "Look, Charlie, I think Bruce would like it better
if you presented it this way . . . Marge, I love you . . .
Joan, I love you . . . it has been called to my attention
that the editor of our shelter magazine . . ." And over
and above it all: "Going down! Down elevator!"
   "Down!" Charlie Gibson yelled from the nadir of
his daze, rushing to the end car, "Down!"
   *God damn it, Janie, don't be such a common little
slut!*

CHAPTER ELEVEN

"WHAT I can't get over," Dudley Q. Davis told Jayne Gibson at noon on March the sixth, "is that it's such a cliché situation."

"I know it," she said, "It's almost as bad as 'thank you for just being Harry.'"

They both nodded somewhat dismally. They stirred their coffees and stared at their cigarettes, remembering that night they had first met—months and months ago—right here in this very restaurant in Greenwich Village. . . .

There had been a rather large group of them—over eight—with no one particularly paired-off, and Jayne and Dudley had sat at the very end of the long table, beside a couple at another table. Neither one had said much to the other, until they had overheard the conversation between the couple.

The woman, a thin, once-pretty, spinsterish type, had obviously been taken to dinner by a salesman for her concern; a large, jolly, flamboyant fellow whose name was Harry.

As they were finishing their dessert, she glanced up at him and said in a sacred tone, "Thank you, Harry."

Harry had guffawed good-naturedly. "For what? For this little old dinner? This is nothing! You don't have to thank me, Florence. This is nothing! Why thank me?"

After a pause, and in that same hallowed tone, the woman responded, "Thank you for just being Harry."

Dudley and Jayne both heard it, and both had the same reaction—a terrible, nearly overwhelming urge to burst into fits of uncontrollable laughter.

102

And 't was while they were restraining themselves, after they had both sensed one another's reaction, that they first looked very deeply into each other's eyes.

And Dudley Q Davis thought: That's a very cute kid across from me.

And Jayne Gibson thought: I bet he has the same sense of humor I do.

And they began talking, talking and laughing, and telling one another about cliché things they had done, said, or overheard. But mostly they only admitted that they had *overheard* them; or that someone had done a certain thing *to them* (been dumb enough to) that was so cliché they were both hysterical thinking about it.

"I remember this girl I was taking out," Dudley had said. "She was a Smith pig. Well, I took her out a couple of times—I don't know—and we necked around, but I was never very serious, and she was. I could tell by her breathing."

"Oh, no! *Really?*"

"Sure you know; huh-huh, huh-huh, huh-huh," Dudley imitated the sound and Jayne Gibson squealed, "Oh, how *aw*-ful! Really?"

"Sure," Dudley said, "but that's not the cliché . . . One night, see, I was kissing her good night, and my mind wasn't exactly on it. Anyway, she realizes this, and she comes out of the clinch and stares up at me with this real dewey-eyed look. She looks at me like that for a while, and then she says, 'Dudley?'

" 'What?' says I.

" 'Dudley,' she says, 'Who hurt you?' That's just what she said, and I said, 'What do you mean?' . . . Well, wait until you hear this. She says, 'Someone hurt you a long time ago, didn't they? *Who hurt you, Dudley?*' . . . Get that, for God's sake. Right out of the soap operas!"

Jayne Gibson hooted, and Dudley slapped his knee three times and threw his head back, laughing.

When the hysteria over that was terminated, Jayne spoke:

"I was out with a fellow once—he was a Yale man, and he was more or less stuck on me, but I just didn't get any message whatsoever from him. Anyway, we'd be together— say for a whole evening, and at some point or other during the evening, when there was a lapse in our conversation, or when we'd been chasing around dancing or running back and forth to the football stadium, he'd suddenly reach for my hand—and in this *doleful* tone—honestly, Dud, I wish you could have *heard* him—he'd say: 'I *miss* you.' . . . Ughhh, I mean—it was *aw*-ful! So gooey!"

More hysteria; then—

"I used to go with a girl like that," Dudley said. "She was from Bennington, I remember. She was always stopping in the middle of something we were doing— in the movies, or restaurants, or even reading out at her summer cottage, and she'd look real coy at me and wrinkle her nose and say, 'Hi!' . . . Oh, God, let me tell you!"

And on and on it went, that night and nights to follow—Dudley Q. Davis and Jayne Gibson, teamed up against the vulgar, the stereotype, the cliché; their accord so perfectly mutual that often around other people they would suddenly became convulsed with this mad laughter that lent magic to their togetherness, and go rushing out of a room, bent double, while the others stared after them murmuring usualities like: "What hit them?"

Or: "Let us in on the joke, too?"

Or: "Must be a private joke."

And still shaking, off and away from the thing that had amused them so hilariously, they looked at one another proudly, with a feeling of utter, unique purity of intelligence and wit and subtle sophistication.

They were a team, and envied as such. Not alone for the fact that Dudley was very tall, extremely handsome

with dark hair, flashing white teeth, and bright blue
eyes; that Jayne was quite short, gamin-beautiful,
and what Dud's colleagues termed "stacked and
packed," and together they created that lovely aura of
physical pulchritude that all such pairs do; but envied too because they seemed to possess some superior
secret unavailable to the commoners, who neither
looked like them, laughed as much as they did, or
seemed so certainly satisfied within the cocoon of their
individual pairs.

Everyone who knew them knew of their love, long
before Jayne Gibson and Dudley Q. Davis knew it.

And everyone would have cried indignantly, "Preposterous!" if they were to know that love between
this splendid couple came as a surprise to both of them;
and that furthermore, neither one had ever been in
love before, not even involved before, the way they
suddenly found themselves that Sunday morning at
Ethel Waterhouse's home in Bala Cynwood, Pennsyl-
vania.

They were week-ending at the Waterhouses, along
with Ethel and Dud's roommate, Myer Forbes, and because naturally both Dudley and Jayne were agnostics
(making certain of the differentiation between that and
an atheist), they didn't go to church. And because
the whole Waterhouse family were staunch Presby-
terians, they all did go—with Myer tagging along too,
reluctantly, dutifully, and somewhat envious at Dud's
and Jayne's having the house to themselves.

"Hi, friend." Dudley suddenly appeared in the doorway to the guest room Jayne was occupying. "I brought
up some coffee and the *Times* crossword. Awake?"

She propped herself up on the pillows (the pillow-
cases and sheets were blue-and-white-striped jobs,
and both she and Dudley remarked: "God, why can't
something remain sacred. Why does everything have
to blossom out in colors and stripes and polka dots?
What's wrong with plain white!") and he sat along-

side her while they sipped coffee and tried to think of
a three-letter word for "the companions of egoes" and
who wrote *Things As They Are.*

Whenever it was that the chemistry between them
first started reacting on them, it did not seem too long
a time to Jayne Gibson, who, without any warning
whatsoever, found herself in the perfectly asinine situation of trying not to breathe so loudly, remembering
Dudley's imitation of the Smith girl—and thinking:
Oh, look now, Jaynie, migirl, let's get a grip on ourselves! But to no avail. She was actually panting,
though Dudley Q. Davis hardly noticed, for right out
of nowhere (or maybe after, out of the corners of his
eyes, he had seen the secret and formidable world of
woman beginning through the sheer part of Jayne's
nylon nightie, there at the top, the pale brown shade
of the nipple's circle, and the soft mound of lovely
white) he found himself faced with the problem of
covering a growth which was not as indigenous to him
as her protrusions were to her, and certainly not anti-
cipated.

"Maybe I ought to get us more coffee," Dudley said
tersely.

She put down the newspaper she had been holding
while they both were figuring out the crossword, and
she said, "Maybe." She said it in such a shy, strange
and odd little voice, that both of them noticed.

"What's wrong?" he said, and his voice too sounded
suspended, somehow, or vaguely hushed.

"Nothing."

"Huh?" He leaned forward a little. "Something
wrong?"

"No," she said, staring into his eyes; their eyes were
glued on one another during this exchange.

"You sound funny."

"I do?"

"Yes."

"I don't know, Dud."

"Is something wrong?"

"No, Dud, I said—"

"You sound funny," he said.

Then he leaned more forward, leaned until his lips brushed hers lightly, and they put their mouths together, gently, feeling their mouths for several slow seconds, their hands not on each other, their arms at their sides, until Dudley Q. Davis lifted his head from hers and said, "Whew!"

"I feel like saying a cliché," she whispered dizzily.

"Don't say anything," he said in a husky voice. "We don't need words."

And so, with the biggest cliché, perhaps, of them all, Dudley Q. Davis made tender, fumbling, but perfectly-satisfying-to-both love with the daughter of Charles Gibson—on the vulgar blue-and-white-striped sheets of the Waterhouses, that Sunday morning when everyone else in the house was listening to a sermon on "The Meaning of Prayer" down at the First Presbyterian Church.

"You always hear about it happening," Dudley told her that, noon, after they had sneaked into New York from Cambridge for the doctor's report, "but you never think that it could happen to you."

She said helplessly, "It's just not that easy to get pregnant. I mean, it's not supposed to be . . . These friends of Daddy's—they tried almost three years. Three years. They used to have to plan the nights they were going to have intercourse. They actually had a schedule for it."

"Yeah," Dudley said, "and the one time we don't plan happens to be the first time, and the first time happens to be the one time."

"I'm sorry," she said.

He said, "It's not your fault."

"Even the restaurant seems—gloomy," she said, looking at the murals of bullfights in Spain, the matadors in their red capes with their heads thrown back as the fierce animals snarled toward them; and around at the neat white-covered tables, the few patrons digging into their paellas, the trays of cocktails passing on trays, and the electric window sign blinking out at the sunny, cold March streets unnecessarily.

"It's better here at night," he said. "Not many people come to the Village at noon to eat. I guess these people here today work around here."

"I was afraid we'd run into my father uptown."

"I know," he said.

"Poor father . . . He'd die if he knew. And after I wrote him that letter telling him about us."

"Stop thinking about it. It doesn't do any good to think about it."

"That sounds like a cliché." She tried to laugh.

"Everything does," Dudley Q. Davis said, "and this will too, Jayne. I love you."

"Oh, and I love you, Dud."

"We're in an awful jam, all right. We should have known something crazy like this would happen to us. We've been so right for each other so far, so perfect. We should have known something would happen."

"Dudley," she said, "what are we going to do? We've got to decide."

"I know it. I'm thinking about it right now. It'll take some phone calls."

"I knew a girl once," she said, "who was three months along and went horseback riding and miscarried. There was something she did with quinine too, but I don't remember that."

Dudley Q. Davis put out his cigarette with an emphatic gesture.

"C'mon," he said, "I have a better idea. Let's get out of here."

"I'll have a dry Rob Roy," Charlie Gibson said to the waiter at the Algonquin; and to Marge, "What'll you have?"

"Nothing," she said.

"No?"

"No, I don't feel like anything."

The waiter went away and Charlie brushed the menu aside and lit a cigarette. He looked very grim. She felt sorry for him, and started to say, "Look, Charlie," but he spoke first.

"It's crowded here this noon."

"Oh, it's always crowded here."

"Seems more than usual."

"Do you think so?" she said, thinking: Maybe just one drink, one very light one to get things going, a Vermouth Cassis, something like that.

Charlie must have read her mind. "Sure you don't want something?" he said.

"No," she said, "I don't feel like anything." Then she said quickly, "Charlie?"

"What?" He looked up at her. He couldn't even make himself smile.

"I've got some news," she said. "I'm resigning from Cadence. I have a better position."

"You're *kidding!*"

"No, I'm not. I've had a good offer somewhere else. You remember Blance Phelan? She's over at Dorset now."

"That's a very good house," Charlie interrupted, his tone picking up. "You're going there?"

"I think it's time I moved along anyway, and it's a wonderful opportunity."

"Marge, I *couldn't* be happier."

"Sooner or later I would have run into trouble at Cadence. It was in the wind . . . And this is really a top opportunity."

"I'm delighted," Charlie said as the waiter put a Rob Roy in front of him.

"You know, I think I'll change my mind after all and have a drink."

"Swell! Want what I'm having?"

"No, something light. I really think I just feel like a rye and soda, not a cocktail."

"Rye and soda," Charlie said. "Will you be working for Blance?"

"We'll be working more or less together. It's a new project that just got out of the talking stage, not even in dummy, so I can't go into it too much with a competitor, *my deah*," she said, and Charlie's laughter was more generous than the incident merited. It was a laugh of relief, she knew, and she felt suddenly heroic and martyred and good . . . and where was her drink?

She said, "It's gratifying to know that I'm still considered tops in my field, even though I am almost as old as Moses. I guess that's what thrills me most of all."

"I can't tell you, Marge—I just can't tell you how pleased I am."

She thought, Yes, you can. It's written all over your face.

"I'll be leaving almost immediately," she said, "even though I probably won't start full time with Dorset for a few months."

"You haven't told Bruce yet, have you?" Charlie asked. It was obvious from his tone that he knew the answer.

"No."

"Gosh I'm happy for you, Marge. I'm very happy."

They beamed at one another momentarily. Then her drink was served.

"Is it a new shelter magazine?"

"Now, now—can't be giving away secrets to the enemy," she answered, picking up the glass, laughing —then feeling the quivering of her hand; she'd purposely ordered a highball knowing she wouldn't be able to handle a long-stemmed cocktail job, but God! Shaking so the ice cubes rattle, glass chattering against my teeth. Does Charlie notice?

Marge Mann laughed. "I have a real case of nerves over this new position."

He grinned, apparently oblivious to the glass and her hands. Then she gulped the whisky, too fast; too much; but got the glass back on the table safely, without incident.

"Say, Charlie, tell me . . . you said you had some news about Jane."

"Oh, God, yes! Yes, it's really turned me inside out." He reached into the inside pocket of his suit, unfolded a letter and passed it across to her. "Why don't you read this? It'll explain it better than I can."

While she was reading it, she noticed that he ordered himself another drink. Well, she didn't want another one anyway; *wanted* it, maybe, but wasn't going to have it; had to play this scene well, didn't want sympathy, didn't want Charlie Gibson thinking, Poor old bag. I ever love *her?* All washed up now; poor old Marge.

In the middle of the letter she laughed.

"What?" he said anxiously.

"This," she said, reading it, "Ezra Pound wrote poetry; poetry called cantoes; that's an interesting piece of news."

"It's that condescending tone all through the letter." Charlie frowned as she continued, watching her face. She could feel his eyes on her and she thought, God, what a brat Charlie has. But she could only half-concentrate on the smug, officious sentiments. She was wondering if Charlie had any inkling at all that she was faking about the job offer, that she was simply trying to make it easy for him, for both of them. And in a way she wished he were at least semisuspicious, not so quickly believing. She finished the letter and put it down between them on the table.

"What do you think of it?" he said.

"She's your flesh and blood, all right."

Charlie was very serious. "What do you mean?"

"Oh, I was more or less joking, Charlie—but she sounds terribly idealistic, in that savagely progressive way of the younger generation, and terribly modern in the same way. I suppose you must have been that way too a little, hmm, when you were in college?"

"I don't know exactly what you're talking about,"
Charlie said.

Marge shrugged, thinking, He's selfish, really selfish.
My God, I'm out on the ash heap, about to become
a problem for the Geriatrics Association and he sits
there worrying about that little brat of his. God, men
are really selfish; no more about Margie this noontime;
all about Janie. He can't even see through my act. Typical, typical.

But aloud she said, "It's hard to describe. What I
mean is—she's probably not any different than you were
at that age; or than I was. Kids don't change
that much from generation to generation. . . ." God,
she wished she had the nerve to get herself another
drink. Why couldn't she just say she felt like having
one—just casually, "Order me another, Charlie."

"I never took anything like an affair so lightly,"
Charlie said. Then he wondered why he felt as though
he shouldn't have said that in front of Marge. After
all, he *had* been in love with her. Poor Marge, pretending she had another job offer with Dorset—poor Marge,
but *good* Marge—typical Marge, taking the burden off
his shoulders, acting as though she didn't give a damn.
She probably had stocks to tide her over; wonderful
the way she actually cared about other people's problems in the face of her own. Well, hell, he'd play
along, never let her know he guessed her game, let
her save face—that was always important to Marge;
she was proud, God love her—and now she was going
to help him solve this riddle that was suddenly Janie.

"Oh, men never take affairs lightly," Marge Mann answered him. "Only women can, but they don't let men
know they can." And that should relieve the twinge
of guilt she sensed he felt the moment he'd said he'd
never taken an affair lightly. Gosh, Charlie was like
an open book. His face told you everything he was
thinking. She had one of those insane impulses to butt
in: "Charlie, I'm on the ash heap. Can't you see beyond
your nose? I'm only acting." But instead she said, "Or-

der me another, Charlie," and her voice sounded immediately calm. Everything was going to be all right —she would sit and listen about Jane and it would be all right now. In the split second between the impulse and the drink order, it had been resolved; she resigned herself.

"Sure," he said, "rye and soda . . . But even in my college days—I swear I can't remember any girl I was ever interested in who took—sex lightly."

"I don't know that Janie's taking it—"

"Wait a minute," Charlie said, "I can so think of one. I sure can! Her name was Mitzie. Mitzie," Charlie said snapping his fingers, frowning. "Mitzie something. God, how could I forget . . ."

MARCH 6, 1957

CHAPTER TWELVE

"WHERE have you been?" she said.

She was sitting under the covers of the bed in the small West Side hotel room, working a crossword and smoking a cigarette. She was dressed in her slip, with a worn-from-too-many-washings cardigan over her shoulders.

Elliot Basescu said, "Walking."

"Uh-huh. That's nice. Nice that you had a walk."

"Walking around Rockefeller Center. Walking around the N.B.S. building. Walking around and thinking."

"Well, you walked right through lunch," she said, "and I'm starved."

She had been pretty once. Now she wasn't. Her black hair was wiry and she had a careless, dowdy appearance. When she smoked a cigarette she smoked it so far down that it invariably burned the tips of her fingers and stained them, and sometimes she never bothered to put them out, but left them cradling in the notch of the ashtray until they were either dead ashes stagnating there, or smoking ashes that had toppled from the notch to the table or the rug, singeing them.

"I'm starved," she repeated as he pulled a manuscript from the briefcase he was carrying. "I hope you're through with that secret project of yours. Is it written in code too?"

"I'm not through with it, as a matter of fact," her husband answered. "I have to cut and add."

"It's so top secret, I hope they're paying top-secret prices."

"Why don't you go out and get some lunch," he said, "if you're starved. I have to finish this."

"Thanks," she said, "I'll always remember New York because we had such a nice time here."

"Why don't you eat over around N.B.S.," he said. "Maybe you'll run into somebody you know."

"Shut up," she said flatly. "Just shut your mouth."

Basescu didn't say anything to that. He opened his typewriter case and set it up on the frail wooden desk.

Slowly she pulled herself out of the bed and wandered across to the bureau. There in a leather frame were the pictures of her son—the baby picture, and the picture of him taken in Korea, where he was killed. She looked at them, her eyes lusterless, and every time she looked at them, even now when Mikie was dead and gone, she wondered what it would have been like if his father had married her—instead of Elliot, and she wondered too *why* Elliot had; he hadn't loved her, that was obvious.

"I'll tell you something else," her husband said as he set paper in the roller of the typewriter. "Charlie Gibson is the executive editor of the magazine house where I was today . . . There, now. What do you think of that?"

"Charlie?" she said incredulously. "Charlie Gibson?"

"Your old flame," he said. "All your old flames seem

to be located in the big city . . . All your old successful flames," he said.

"I was so sure Charlie'd be a writer," she said, leaning against the bureau with her back to it, in an idle,
lazy fashion. "I was almost positive."

"You were always positive, about the wrong things
and the wrong people." He set his margins and lit a
cigarette.

"I wasn't wrong about Charlie. He was wonderful
to me—always—just wonderful. I hurt Charlie a lot."

"But *you* didn't get hurt."

"Not by Charlie Gibson."

"And *I* didn't get hurt."

"Okay, Elliot—we both got hurt. You became a martyr
and I became a mother. What do you want me to do,
go over to N.B.S. and kill him! Take a gun in my purse
and blow his brains out because he wouldn't marry
me . . . Aren't you ever going to forget him?"

She turned around and opened a bureau drawer. She
took out a garter belt and stockings and slammed the
drawer shut.

Basescu said calmly, "I don't want you to do anything. In the long run he'll be discovered for what he
is."

"Oh, please," she said, bending to roll a stocking
up her leg, "don't start that hogwash again. If he's
a fairy, I'm a Lesbian . . . He's got a family now, you
know—and kids! Legal and all. Please, don't start *that*
again, Elliot!"

"What about that Chicago incident?"

"That's your yellow-journal scuttlebutt. You never
printed it. How come you never printed it if it was
news?"

"*I* would have printed it," Elliot Basescu said.

"I can believe that."

"It was all verified," he said. "Don't worry. Some day
the story will be told."

"Oh, sure."

"I told you how he ran after me; the propositions

he made to me. I was a nervous wreck. I was very sensitive and he made a nervous wreck out of me; nearly sent me to a psycho ward. I told you that."

"Sure," she said, hooking the garter belt, "you told me. You told me you married me to get away from him, to feel like a man again. You told me that night out by the columns when we both got drunk, you had to feel like a man again—because of him. Sure, you told me."

"Mike could have been mine as well as his. I still believe that," Basescu answered.

"Mike could have been anyone's," she said. "After that night in your room with Charlie, I didn't give a damn. He could have been anyone's, but he happened to be his. And you know it . . . And whatever all this other stuff is about Avery being a queer, I don't know." She straightened up, adjusted her seams, then said, "But I *do* know you're a little preoccupied with the subject."

"I've got to finish this work," he said. "Aren't you going out for lunch?"

"And I do know," she said, "that you were at it again last night."

"Go on to lunch," he said. "Go walk by N.B.S. Maybe you'll meet somebody you know."

"Whenever you're at it, you bring home scores of matchboxes. One from every place, huh? Happy hunting, huh?"

"Go on to lunch," he said. "They've got a lot of nice places over in Rockefeller Center."

"Got some money?" she said, grabbing her coat from the edge of the bed.

"My wallet's on the table," he grunted. Then he looked up from his typewriter, frowned, and shook his head slowly. "That's funny!"

"What?" She took out two dollars.

"I was just going to say, 'Why don't you go over to Times Square and get your voice recorded for Mike.

He'd love it.' I was just going to say that. Isn't it funny?"

She stood in the doorway. "Yeah," she said slowly, sighing, "I know. I've been thinking a lot of him too this trip. All those things he bought the week he was here after High."

"I knew they made records over there and I was just going to say it. That's the funniest thing," he said.

Neither of them said anything for a moment. She looked at the rug worn threadbare beneath her, and he stared at the walls.

"Golly," he said, "makes you feel funny."

"I know," she said, "I know . . . Well, see you later, El. Don't work too hard."

"Okay, Mitz," he murmured. "See you."

MARCH 6, 1957

CHAPTER THIRTEEN

BRUCE CADENCE was an uncomplicated sort of fellow once one knew what made him tick.

He was a "follow-through" man. He could follow through on anything, better than anyone, but he could never start anything himself. He was like a car who needed a push to get going, and any time he had ever tried to begin on his own, he only flooded his motor with his impulsive enthusiasm, and stalled, and had to wait for the old reliable push again.

He had married Mildred Cadence shortly after they had been graduated from high school, even though he had barely spoken to her at all during their four years of classes together. He had noticed her and liked her, but he had never been an aggressive person, nor an original one, nor very confident either—unless someone put the firecracker under him; then he could go like hell.

Mildred's firecracker was something she wrote in his school yearbook: "I'm the girl who ruined your book by writing upside down."

She hadn't intended it as a firecracker. As a matter of fact, she had deliberately debated what on earth to write in his book, because he was so mild-mannered and she hardly knew him, and she couldn't just gush across the page as she did with others. So she chose a frivolous sentiment.

But to Bruce Cadence it was clever, eye-drawing, amusing, and ironic.

Bruce Cadence called her up and asked her out, and four weeks later found himself riding beside her on a train to Niagara Falls, wondering what on earth he was going to do with her once the door slammed behind them in the little hotel for honeymooners there.

But Cadence needn't have worried, for Mildred was swept off her feet by this quiet boy who had given her a whirlwind courtship and proposed to her on top a roller coaster. He had burst into tears when she accepted, then gagged and vomited once they got on solid ground again, but took her arm gently and announced: "We'll have to wait three days. It's the law. Come on, we'll tell your father."

Without framing it with words in her mind, Mildred understood what made him tick—if not during the courtship, certainly on that wedding night, after they had lain beside one another quietly in the double bed that smelled vaguely of mildew—and she had taken the initiative by reaching for his hand under the covers and, quite tenderly, squeezing it . . . . He was a follow-through man; once someone started him, Bruce Cadence went like hell.

Bruce Cadence needed no one besides Mildred in his life apart from Cadence Publications. He relied wholly upon her, and found her wholly reliable; and consistently reliable. But in his business microcosm he found his partners less faithful, a little fickle, and not altogether comprehensible to him in their sundry moods and metamorphoses.

Charlie Gibson's metamorphosis, for example, bewildered Cadence because he had always depended upon Gibson, not merely for business ideas, but for business deals—ethics and integrity. He respected Charlie's opinion, not alone because it could sell magazines in Duluth, but also because it could sell them tastefully. Taste was Charlie's word.

"It's not in good taste," he used to say, or, "I don't care about sales figures, Bruce, it's in very bad taste!"

And while he "told" Bruce Cadence what he thought, while he raged at him over a certain issue that was unsettled between them—Charlie's language, conduct, Charlie himself, was never in good taste; but he was always effective, usually right, and nearly always convincing.

Bruce Cadence kept thinking of that as he faced Wally Keene across his desk, after he had come back from lunch. He had come back to find Sandy in tears, with her coat on, and her announcement that she was leaving for the afternoon, "and maybe for good."

It had upset Cadence enormously. He had followed his secretary to the elevator, attempting to reason with her, or at least discover the reason for her sudden fit; and as she had gotten on, oblivious to his pleas, Keene had gotten off.

The elevator door shut, and Cadence was face to face with Keene, whose countenance was tipped with an amused grin.

"Bull pen hysteria," Keene remarked. "It's a form of regression. Take a girl out of the office bull pen and make her an executive secretary, but in times of crisis, she's still the little file girl who went home in tears because the business manager gave her hell for chewing the erasers off the ends of pencils."

"This isn't funny," Cadence had snapped. He walked

ahead of Keene, with Keene following him into his office.

Cadence said, "I wish I knew what upset her so. I think it was my firing Marge."

"It's upset everyone for different reasons," Keene answered. "She's a great mother figure, and you're something of a father figure, leastwise where Miss Scott is concerned."

"I don't know what the hell you're talking about."

"Well," Keene said cryptically, "would you like it if *your* father tossed your mother out of the house? It's a very threatening situation."

"Are you going to one of those head doctors, Wally?"

"Yes," Keene said, pulling a leather chair aside and sitting in it as Bruce sat down at his desk, "and it's amazing how much insight a fellow gets about things . . . Do you know, Bruce, I was actually feeling guilty about firing old Marge, the office Hecuba. Until I figured out it was simply displacement."

"I can't say I felt very happy about it either."

"Maybe *you* should visit my doctor."

"I don't need a doctor to make me happy about something that's unfortunate."

"But it might not be as unfortunate as you think. People get pretty much what they deserve in this world."

Bruce Cadence said, "I don't believe that, Wally. Particularly in business. I think they often get what they ask for, and they often find out too late that it isn't what they want—but it doesn't mean they necessarily deserve it. And that reminds me—"

Keene interrupted to say, "All philosophy is psychosemantic; just words. Psychology is tangible, scientific. And I still say, people get what they deserve."

"All right, as you like, Wally. What's bothering me is: does Cadence deserve the *Vile* dummy?"

Keene crossed his legs and lit a cigarette. "The answer is no. That's why we're putting it out as a bastard book."

"But it's ours."

"We don't dignify it with our name."

"Exactly! It's a bastard. I don't know that I approve of being responsible for bastards in any form." Cadence got up and began his pacing back and forth across the thick maroon rug, an Uppman caught between his chubby fingers. "I kept your appointment with Basescu this morning."

"And *he* bothers you. That's it, eh?"

"The article too. It'll ruin Avery."

"He deserves it," Keene said, sucking in on his cigarette. "Look, Bruce, that guy went after a kid in Chicago! We've got proof, right out of police files! You saw it! He got off; beat the rap—like that." Keene snapped his fingers. "Do you think that's right?"

"Of course not!"

"Avery's getting what he deserves!"

"He may deserve some sort of punishment—"

"Some sort of punishment!" Keene exclaimed.

"Well, he may deserve to be punished, but is it our business to deal it out and capitalize on it? That's my point, Keene!"

Wally Keene got up and faced Cadence. "Look, Bruce," he began, "are you proud of *Topic?*"

"It's our best book, saleswise."

"No, I mean are you proud of it?"

"Yes. Yes, it's done a lot of big things recently. The story on the new vaccine, for example."

"And how about the one on that ex-Nazi who was working for the occupation forces? The one who ordered his men to save the heads of corpses with good teeth, so he could make paperweights out of their skulls and give them to friends!"

"Y-yes," Cadence said thoughtfully. "It was a good article. We got newspaper mention on it, world-wide. But that's a little different, Wally—"

"Wait a minute. Is it?" Keene bent and tamped out his cigarette in the ashtray, then straightened himself,

facing Cadence. "We gave that guy exactly what he
deserved."

"Charlie was behind that story. He pushed hard for
that one. I remember."

"Sure, he did!" Keene said. "That article was one of
the reasons I wanted to work for Cadence. I thought,
'There's a house that has some zeal, not a namby-pamby today-we'll-make-flower-baskets-out-of-old-straw-hats
slick house, but a house with guts! And, Bruce, wasn't
that an exposé? Didn't we deal out the punishment in
that case, too? And sure, we made money on it—but
it wasn't dirty money. That Nazi bastard deserved it!"

Cadence scratched his head, silent as he walked back
behind his desk and sank into his leather swivel chair.

Wally said, "What's the difference between him and
Avery?"

"There's a difference between a homosexual and a
murderer, Wally."

"A pederast is a murderer in a sense. Picking on kids!
Do you know what a thing like that can do to a kid?
. . . Sure, there's a difference in degree, but Otto Avery
still deserves to get his tail fixed!"

"*Topic* wouldn't touch the story," Cadence said.

"All right, so what, Bruce? *Topic* isn't as hard-hitting
a book as *Vile* . . . And *Topic* was in the red last month,
wasn't it, for all its sales-power."

"Yes," Cadence said, sighing, rubbing his forehead.
"We really need a life saver at this point . . . I don't
know—"

"If anyone around here has a better idea," Keene
said, "I'd be interested."

Bruce Cadence said, "So would I."

Keene stood up. "Who has the dummy now?"

"Charlie."

"He hasn't okayed it yet?"

"I've been keeping him busy with the detective line,
but he's promised to shoot it up to me this afternoon
. . . Basescu says Charlie went to school with Avery."

"I know."

"I wonder what Charlie's reaction will be on the story."

"According to Elliot, Charlie hated him . . . But remember, Bruce," Wally said, "whatever his reaction is, that's our lead story, our cover piece!"

"I know, I know."

"And anything Charlie has to say will be colored by the little duty he had to perform."

"Firing Marge, you mean . . . I don't even know when he plans to do it."

"Or *if*," Wally Keene said. "People are complicated mechanisms, Bruce. You can't discount psychology in any circumstance. Charlie's going to feel very guilty over having to fire a former affair."

"I should have done it myself," Cadence said, "only Charlie's the one who hires and fires. I didn't want to make a special case out of Marge. That might have been twice as bad."

"I wouldn't worry if I were you. Worry is just displacement anyway."

"I might *have* to visit your doctor," Cadence grunted, "just to find out what the hell you're talking about."

Wally laughed, and started toward the door. Then he stopped momentarily. He said, "Hope Miss Scott comes back. It's tough to train a new girl."

"I don't understand it at all," Bruce said.

"Very simple, boss—the child's in love with you."

"Hogwash!" Bruce Cadence snorted. "I'm old enough to be her father."

"That's the point." Keene laughed.

He waved and went out.

Bruce Cadence sat thinking, and his thoughts kept returning to Charlie. In a sense, what he felt was that Charlie had deserted him, deserted him from the day he had made him Executive Editor and hired Keene, and Bruce resented it. It made him indignant, not just as an employer who had rewarded an employee for his diligence by promoting him—only to find he rested on his laurels as a result—but also as a colleague of Charlie's, who found after years of camaraderie, a withholding on Charlie's part, a tightening, a gradual growing away.

And for what reason, Cadence could not fathom.

He thought of that—and then he thought of Sandy's running out on him, and the next thought he had was that here he was deserted by the two people he relied on most, and left with a man who trotted off to a head-shrinker three times a week; left, literally, with a nut! A smart nut, no doubt about it, but nevertheless, a nut! . . . That was exactly how Cadence felt about these couch-goers that were becoming more and more prevalent. It used to be that employees asked for time off to see a dentist, or a doctor (a *real* doctor, Cadence thought), or to go to a funeral. But in recent years, some of his executives, in particular, began explaining their absence from their offices with the fact they were at their psychiatrists; until Bruce put a stop to it by making it clear in a memo that employees were not allowed time off to see doctors unless it was an emergency, and unless it was a *physical* sickness, emergency or not.

As a matter of fact, Cadence couldn't even talk comfortably with Keene—not the way he used to talk with Charlie. Somehow he and Keene would sit down and discuss something like reorganizing distribution in the Southwest, and end up on the subject of incest.

Bruce Cadence wasn't even sure what the hell incest was. Something about wanting to sleep with your parents, and Jesus H. Christ, what kind of a person wanted to do *that!*

He didn't know anyone who did and he didn't want to know anybody who did, and if Wally Keene did, he didn't want to know that.

Maybe all the young men today were Keenes. Cadence didn't know. He only knew he liked the Charlies in this world—the men who wrestled with real problems: how to break off an affair, how to get a raise, how to pay for a house that was more expensive than one could afford, how to improve a bridge game or break 70 on the golf course, where to send his kids to school, how to lose weight, and what the hell to take for a hangover!

By God, Cadence thought, I'm going to call Charlie up here and tell him how I feel, and ask him how he feels, by God. Should have thought of that before.

And first, I'll get Wadley and Smythe on the phone and send some flowers off to Sandy.

The old ways are the best. I don't know tricks. Not going to sit here feeling hurt . . . What would Keene call me? A machinist or masonist or some damn psychological hogwash.

While he was sitting there thinking these thoughts, he suddenly became aware of the noise off in the background outside his office, the persistent clatter of a typewriter which meant Sandra Scott was busy typing up the morning's dictation.

He threw back the intercom switch and said, "I'm glad you're back, Sandy."

"I'm sorry about the temper tantrum, Mr. Cadence."

"I guess we're all entitled to one now and then . . . Now let's see if we can get Charlie back."

MARCH 6, 1957

CHAPTER FOURTEEN

ON THE way back from lunch, Charlie Gibson got the idea to call Joan and invite her into the city for dinner.

Marge had said something over lunch that was so obvious it was a wonder he had not thought of it himself: that of course Joan should help him decide what to do about Janie, that despite Janie's fervent request that her mother be left out of the matter, it was Joan's problem too.

Marge had sounded bored when she had made the suggestion, and an equally obvious fact struck Charlie suddenly—that she *was* bored, that it wasn't her province to help him with this sort of problem at all, that she had just faced and solved a problem of her own, and she was probably even a little disdainful of Charlie's inability to cope with the matter quietly and with orderliness, as she had handled hers.

He had to admire Marge Mann; he did admire her. She was strong and proud and certain; and she rolled with the punch. If there were any lesson in life Charlie would want Janie to learn and learn well, it would be pride—pride in herself, no matter what happened, the pride of independence.

In a sense, Janie's mother was. But Joan's confidence was wild and went barreling along on wheels, while Marge's stood firm on good ground. Joan was a raving optimist; Marge, a pleasant pessimist. Charlie decided the latter needed people less, and he supposed that was one reason Marge had never married anyone and one reason he hadn't married Marge.

He didn't want Janie to be the extreme independent spirit Marge Mann was, but he couldn't help hoping she was a little less dependent than her mother, for Charlie Gibson had always had the misconception that his wife was a vulnerable and fragile, emotionally, as a piece of Chinese porcelain—when it concerned Charlie.

He could remember little things that had happened long ago. A day, for instance, when he sat on the Yacht Club dock up in Auburn, New York, and told her how much he had loved Mitzie Thompson. He could remember glancing down at her once and seeing her face, reading her thoughts, and thinking to himself, The poor kid's afraid no one will ever want to marry her the way I wanted to marry Mitzie. She was a terribly skinny, bony kid and Charlie felt sorry for her.

Sure, it was ironic; but more than once after they were married, Charlie felt the main reason he had proposed to her was that he felt so bad about taking her out in the car that night and halfway undressing her. He was ten years older than she was, after all; and he had taken advantage of her, scared her silly; because when he'd exclaimed, "What's happening to us?" her whispered "I don't know" had haunted Charlie for weeks and weeks after. He felt almost like a child molester, and he was certain she had cried herself to sleep that night after he'd dropped her at her house.

It was hard, after so many years, to think back on things with any real lucidity, but there were two things Charlie had done to Joan for which he never forgave himself.

One was that he had, in his rage at the announcement she was pregnant, accused her of planning the baby. Despite all anyone could tell him about a woman's diaphragm being, on occasion, not altogether reliable, particularly if it had been a misfit, he had persisted in his accusation for months. It was a wonder to him Janie was born healthy, a wonder and a marvel and a joy. So he never forgave himself that.

The other thing was, of course, Marge.

At least Joan never had to know about it. Thank God.

She would have left him, simply left him, and she wouldn't have gotten over it, like some women. She wouldn't have married another man and started all over again; she simply would have grown old, bitter, and probably blighted Janie's whole outlook. Well, thank God it never happened. It took a war to make Charlie know whom he wanted to go home to and it was an odd thing that, during the war, actually during some of the rough moments when he wondered if he'd come out alive, and whom he'd want to see, Marge would come to mind. He'd think, Marge ought to be here, by rights, fighting for me. She always fought my other battles, and won; bet she'd slaughter these Nips.

And he'd remember the way Joan's naked body felt, all curled around him, hanging on to him like a tame boa, when she slept. And sometimes she'd whimper in her sleep. And he'd murmur, "That's all right, I'm here!" He remembered things like that—and then he'd remember the shoes.

They were living on Bleecker Street that Christmas, in the cold-water railroad flat. They were broke—because Charlie's first job in New York paid next to nothing. He'd just suffered through some preposterous ailment called mononucleosis which had cost them an arm and a leg in doctor's bills, and Joan was in her fourth month.

To complicate things, Charlie first fell in love with his wife that month. Before, he had only loved her, but now he was honest-to-God *in love* with the woman he married, and between them they had four dollars to splurge on Christmas.

They called it their "Gift of the Magi" Christmas afterwards, because Charlie spent his two on a very sexy-smelling cologne from Liggett's, which gave her hives; and she spent her two getting his best shoes resoled (they were stuffed with cardboard before she whipped them off to the cobbler's). And she was inordinately proud of the fact she had talked the cobbler, not only into new soles, but also into taps for both the heels and the toes for only two dollars. At the office where Charlie worked, he was known as Mr. Astaire. But he never told her that; he just sat around the house wondering why she didn't realize men didn't wear taps on their toes and heels, and wondering, as well, what was making her itch herself all the time.

For a long time he carried in his wallet the note she had written with the shoes: "I'll never let you touch ground, darling!" until ultimately someone picked his pocket.

And Joan saved the little note he wrote: "To my very sexy mother" until it suddenly dawned on him

one day years later, as he was searching through a
bureau drawer for a collar button, and came across
the note, that it was more odious than facetious—in
the light of Freud and the Forties; and he'd put a match
to it.

When Charlie stepped into the drugstore on the
corner to call Joan immediately, before she called in
her market list, he got a busy signal; and he decided
something else about the difference between Marge
and Joan. Joan was a blabbermouth; God, she blabbed
everything! Everything, and to everyone! She was probably on the phone right now blabbing out another in-
stallment in the life history of Mrs. Charles Gibson, to
Aileen Tullett, her worst competition in the blabbermouth contest. Maybe he'd *never* get through to her.
Not all afternoon. Maybe he should send a wire.

Now Marge Mann was a lot of things, but she was
not a sob sister, and she was not a woman's woman.
She was a *man's* woman, and the reason was that she
could keep her mouth shut and not tell herself all over
the place.

That's something else Janie should learn, Charlie
thought— Writing a letter to announce she was having
an affair! She got *that* from Joan.

Then the rather incongruous thought flashed through
his mind: but where the hell would I be if she were
doing it without my knowing it? I wouldn't even be
able to advise her. It wouldn't occur to me Jane would
let some young buck—not *Jane*. Jayne?

When Charlie got back to his office, he told Bonnie
to put in a call for Mrs. Gibson. He reread Janie's
letter twice. Then, dutifully but in a haphazard sort of
way, he shuffled through the papers on his desk, and
out from under them, pulled the *Vile* dummy.

Splashed across the front of the mock cover were
the words:

OTTO AVERY KEEPS IT GAY!

Charlie didn't get it right away. His only reaction

was, "Don't tell me that bastard makes interesting
copy."

Then he turned to the fourth page and read the blurb
on the story: *FROM COAST TO COAST OUR FA-
VORITE COMMENTATOR HAS BEEN MAKING
NEWS THAT HE DOESN'T DARE REPORT, BE-
CAUSE IT SOUNDS TOO MUCH LIKE A FAIRY
STORY.*

Very slowly now, Charlie Gibson began to read the
copy.

The woman in the phone booth at the Algonquin
Hotel was very drunk. Two bellboys lingered along
the outside.

"It's a wonder she can dial the number," one said.

"She can't," the other said. "She's tried three times.
. . . There, she's got it now."

"It's a wonder she can remember the number. It's a
wonder she can stand up!"

"She can't," his companion said. "She's leaning a-
gainst the wall."

"I'll bet she gets the wrong number."

"No, she's talking."

"It could still be the wrong number. I know a dame
used to get herself loaded and go call up the Weather
and just sound off like crazy, giving the Weather hell.
And all the time the Weather would be playing over
and over, 'Cloudy skies forecast for Monday; strong
winds,' and this babe would be in there hollering, 'You're
a son of a bitch, do you hear! You're a son of a bitch!'
Over and over. It was the craziest thing I ever knew."

"Listen," the other one said. "She's talking."

"Bet she's calling Weather."

"Listen!"

From inside the booth the voice whined:

"Come over here and talk to me . . .

"No, I am *not* drunk. You believe that rumor? Hah-h!
Et tu, Brutus? Eh? . . .

"I wouldn't ask you to if it weren't important! . . .

"Can't wait until *five!* . . .

"If you don't come to me, I'll come to you . . .

"What do you mean *you* wouldn't do that. I'm talking about what *I'd* do. And I'll come to you if you don't come to me . . .

"No, right now! . . .

"No! . . .

"I have *not* been drinking, and I will not get in a cab and go home and hear from you later! . . .

"No! . . .

"Yes, I do need to see you! I need to! I need to! . . .

"Yes . . .

"Yes, right away . . .

"Yes, thank you, yes . . .

"G'by! . . .

When the woman came out of the phone booth, the pair of bellboys ducked to one side.

She said, "Listening huh?"

"No, ma'am," one said.

The other said, "What do you think of this weather we've been having?" And he nudged his companion sharply in the ribs with his elbow.

The woman looked at them for a moment, weaving slightly.

Then she said, "Boys, I want you to know something."

"Yes, ma'am?"

"Boys," she said, "you are looking at a barren woman!"

"Where are you going?" Bonnie asked as Charlie Gibson rushed past her. "Wait a second. I've got Mrs. Gibson on one wire, and Mr. Cadence on the other."

"Tell Mrs. Gibson I'll call her back," he said, "and tell Bruce—tell him to go to hell!"

"When will you be back?" she called at Charlie. "He'll want to know about the dummy. What'll I tell him?"

"Tell him what I told you to!" Charlie snapped. Then he disappeared around the corner.

His secretary stared blankly at the empty space he had just occupied. Then, shaking herself to efficiency, she pressed the button down on Cadence's call.

"He just stepped out for a moment, Mr. Cadence," she said. "He said he'll call you back. . . . Well, of course he knew who was calling," and, flustered, added quickly, "Well, no, maybe he *didn't*. I mean, I'm not sure, Mr. Cadence. It's all very confusing here today. I mean, it's Mr. Gibson's birthday."

Then, she finished: "I don't suppose it has *anything* to do with it, sir," and heard the click in her ear.

MARCH 6, 1917

CHAPTER FIFTEEN

ON THE morning of Charlie Gibson's thirteenth birthday, he had set fire to the draperies in the living room of the Gibson home on South Street in Auburn, New York.

It was done deliberately, about an hour after breakfast.

At breakfast, Charlie's father had appeared with two huge birthday-wrapped packages, and Charlie had sat in delightful suspense beside his younger brother, Gus, ten, who was already taller than Charlie, and who could knock Charlie down when he wanted to. And he wanted to a lot of times.

Charlie's father had said in his gruff tone: "Someone in this house has a birthday today. Now who would that be?" and stood at the head of the table holding the gifts.

"It's me," Charlie had answered.

"It's *I*," his father had corrected him. "All right then, come and claim your gift."

Charlie pushed his chair back and went to his father, reaching out for the packages. His father handed him only one.

"The other is for Gussie," he told Charlie.

"It's not *his* birthday."

"Well, we got him something anyway," Charlie's father said. "He'll want to celebrate your birthday too."

"I never got anything on his!"

"Listen to me, yong man," the senior Gibson said, "you're very nearly in danger of not getting anything on your own! . . . Now pass this package to your brother."

Charlie's gift was the huge model sailboat which he had always wanted; and Gussie's was a fire engine.

The fire Charlie set was wholly successful; it blazed. The newly-qualified fireman in the Gibson family was occupied, at the time, with mole-hunting in a vacant lot several blocks away, and Charlie's father was off in the library reading the newspaper and grunting over the results of the Versailles Peace Treaty. Charlie's mother smelled the smoke from the kitchen, and appeared in the living room just in time to witness the flames' final swallowing of the blueberry-print fabric, and to scream, "Fire! Matthew! Oh, my God!"

Matthew Gibson's reaction was one of tired resignation at the fact he had uncannily fathered a frightful misfit. Thank heaven for Gussie, anyway. And he had walloped with his belt, fined him one dollar, to be paid from his allowance of ten cents a month, and taken his sailboat back to Sears Roebuck.

Amelia Gibson had hunted six months for that blueberry print, and she was less resigned. She marched her son into the kitchen, struck a match, and forced his hand under the flames.

"You hurt those draperies just like this hurts," she said bitterly.

"Draperies aren't alive," he told her in a reasonable tone. Then he began to feel the heat. She kept his hand there, and Charlie ultimately broke one of the resolutions for his thirteenth year he had scribbled in the flyleaf of his Bible: "Beginning this year I will never cry in my life again."

Charlie spent the afternoon of his thirteenth birthday in his room, his hand wrapped in gauze and Unguentine, reading Kipling's poem *If*, over and over:

> *If you can keep your head when all about you*
> *Are losing theirs and blaming it on you . . .*

His father worried himself with business problems down at the Gibson Mayonnaise factory.

And Gussie Gibson took the wheels off his engine and put them back on again.

Only Amelia Gibson and Charlie seemed to brood over the incident, and at nine o'clock that evening, as Charlie was putting on his pajamas, his mother appeared in his room.

"How's your hand, Charlie?" she wanted to know.

Charlie shrugged.

"It was a bad burn," she said. "I want you to do something for me."

"What?"

"Come here," she said.

Charlie went over to where she was sitting on his bed. He watched, puzzled, as she took a match out from the pocket of her dress.

"Light it," she said.

"Why?"

"Do as I say," she said.

Charlie lit the match and his mother held her hand out to it. Instantly, Charlie pulled the match away.

"All right," she said. "We'll do it over. I have more matches. We'll do it until it's right."

"*Why?*" Charlie protested.

His mother ordered, "Strike the match, Charlie. Do as I tell you!"

A dozen burnt matches later Amelia Gibson's hand was as severely burned as her son's, and she left the room in stony silence.

Charlie put the light out and lay in the dark wondering why she just couldn't have said that she was sorry.

MARCH 6, 1957

CHAPTER SIXTEEN

She was waiting for him in the bar.

"Hi, papa-doodle," she said. "Pull up a toadstool."

"What's the trouble?" he said, sitting down. To the bartender he said, "Double Scotch, neat."

"No trouble. I'm celebrating, papa-doodle. Can't a gal celebrate?"

"I've only got time for one, Marge. This is a hell of a frantic day!"

"All upset over Janie, huh, papa-doodle?"

"Not just that. That *Vile* dummy too. I just read it."

"Juicy?"

"*Very!* . . . But what's *your* trouble?"

"I don't got no troubles, papa-doodle. I'm celebrating. Told you I was celebrating."

"I'm not in the celebrating mood, I'm afraid."

Charlie took a good swallow of the Scotch the bartender set before him.

"Who'd they smear, papa-doodle?"

"The lead article's on a fellow I went to college with. Otto Avery."

"You never told me you went to college with old: 'This is the news and my views on the news'" she said, imitating Avery's clipped baritone.

"The article says he's queer."

"Is he?"

"Hard to believe. There certainly isn't anything feminine about him."

"Don't be naive, papa-doodle. Some of the best stallions I ever pulled out my hide-a-bed for were fruits. Didn't look it, but were . . . Get me another rye, huh?"

"How many have you had?"

"I'm not a counter, papa-poodle. Why count? Will it make you rich?"

"A rye," Charlie said. He swallowed the rest of his shot. "I might as well have another too. A single, neat, this time."

"He's cute, isn't he, papa-doodle? The bartender?"

"Adorable."

"When *Vile* does an exposé of Margie, I got the perfect title. Call it 'The Bartended.' Huh?"

"It's all documented," Charlie said, "and I suppose even Keene wouldn't risk a possible lawsuit, but—" He took a swig of the new drink.

"But what?"

"I wonder where Keene dug up the facts? Wonder who wrote it?"

"Ask him, papa-doodle."

"Keene? The hell with it! The whole thing's in lousy taste! I don't know why Bruce can't see that."

"He's bewitched, maybe. Maybe Bruce and he are queer. Huh?" She chortled.

Charlie frowned and rubbed his forehead. "I wish I could think back and remember things clearly. What Avery was actually like."

"It's hard to think back clearly. I can't even remember what *we* were like. Were we ever us, papa-doodle?"

"In one part the writer said Avery bribed some boy in our frat house to have relations with him. It rings a bell and it doesn't. Gosh, it's funny how your memory slips away."

"All our yesterdays, huh, papa-doodle?"

"I just remember Avery was a bastard. I'd gone to prep school with him for a year or so too. I don't remember much about him then, except I never liked him. In college we dated the same girl. Avery got her pregnant, so the rumor went, but he wouldn't marry her. Some other guy did." Charlie snapped his fingers. "That was Mitzie Thompson—the girl I mentioned at lunch today, remember?"

"All I remember about lunch, papa-doodle," she said, "is that you were afraid to can me."

Charlie swallowed his drink and looked at her. "I wasn't afraid to, Marge. I was reluctant to."

"But I saved you from the fire, didn't I, papa-doodle."

"You don't have the other job, eh? I didn't think so."

"It was a beautiful gesture though, wasn't it?"

"It *was*, Marge, up until I walked in here."

"I'm not going to spoil it. You see me crying in my beer or anything?"

"I wouldn't blame you if you did."

"Not *me*, papa-doodle. I'm a Spartan."

"What do you think you'll do?"

"Take an extended vacation, papa-doodle. Florida, California, who knows?"

"Then your finances are in good shape?"

"Everything's shipshape, Captain."

"I'm glad to hear it, Marge. It was a rotten break."

"Thanks to Mr. Keene, tracer of lost persons."

"With enough rope, Keene's going to hang himself. And he'll hang Cadence too. This *Vile* thing is going to drag us right down. Bruce'll see soon enough."

"Why don't you go up and tell him like you used to, papa-doodle?"

"Why the hell should I? Keene's his troubleshooter."

"I can remember how good you used to be in the hay after you went up and told Bruce off. 'Member?"

"Un-uh," Charlie said.

"Was I good in the hay, Charlie?"

"Sure, Marge. You were swell in the hay."

"You ever remember it, Charlie?"

"Sure I remember it."

"I mean, do you ever think of it and wish for it back?"

"I don't know," Charlie said. He swallowed his Scotch. "What the hell, I'm going to have another!"

He signaled to the bartender.

"Well, *do* you?"

"Do I what?"

"Ever think of it and wish for it back?"

"What's the point in discussing it, Marge?"

"I just want to know, is all, papa-doodle."

"I don't reminisce much any more."

She said, "You didn't go to bat for me, did you, Charlie?"

"It was all decided. I got the memo this morning."

"Lots of times things were decided that you undecided for Bruce, papa-doodle."

"He wouldn't have listened to me, Marge. Keene is the new fair-haired boy around Cadence."

"You didn't even try, did you?"

"No," Charlie said. "I didn't."

"Did you agree with the decision? Was that it, papa-doodle?"

"No, Marge, I didn't *agree* with the decision. I think it was a lousy decision, like all of Keene's are."

"You used to speak up in the old days. No matter what."

"I'm getting old," Charlie said. "Today's my birthday."

"Is it the sixth of March, no kidding?"

"It's the sixth of March," Charlie said. "I'm fifty."

"Buy you a drink, papa-doodle?"

"I ought to go back."

"C'mon and have another, hmm?"

"How many have you had? I can never tell whether you've had too many."

"You never could, Charlie. There are a lot of things you never could tell about me . . . Hey, bartender!"

It was after that drink, and another, and going on four o'clock when Charlie glanced at his watch and thought: Jesus Christ, I've got to get back! and she said suddenly:

"Charlie, I'm a barren woman."

"I have to go," he said. "Really!"

"Do you know what it's like to be wheeled into a room a woman, and a coupla hours later to be wheeled out a nothing?"

"You're drunk," he said. "You don't know what you're talking about any more."

"Oh, yes, I do, papa-doodle. I'm talking about my hysterectomy. My operation, papa-doodle. They pilfered my ovaries back last Christmas, d'you know that?"

"You said it was a check-up."

"Well, it wasn't. They wheeled me in a woman and they wheeled me out a nothin', papa-doodle. I'm fini!"

"I'm sorry," he said.

"Oh, I know what you're thinking. You're thinking, Well, she's only an old bag that stopped having the curse back in the year one, so what the hell. But you're wrong, papa-doodle. Did you know that? I was a medical miracle; still flowing at fifty-nine!"

"Fifty-nine?"

"Don't look it, do I, papa-doodle?"

"No," he said. "Look, Marge, I—"

"Now, you just sit still, papa-doodle. I hadda sit through a whole lunch and listen about Janie losing her virginity, and you can just as well sit over a drink and hear about Margie losin' her ovaries. It's a little more important than what Janie lost—got to lose that 'ventually anyway. But, Charlie—" Her voice caught for the first time. Charlie stared at her. "You're a woman till they bury you if you got your God-damned ovaries," she went on. "But once they're gone, you're dead. You're on the ash-heap. Fini! . . . Charlie, listen, I'm coming apart, Charlie. All the sawdust is coming out."

"Why didn't you tell me, Marge? About all of this?"

"What could you have done, papa-doodle? Get me another pair?"

"I don't know that I could have done much more than talk with you, but that would have helped. I would have wanted to be able to help you that way."

"I couldn't. I'm not that way, papa-doodle. I'm from the pull-yourself-up-by-your-own-boot-straps-school. 'Member?"

"I'm sorry, Marge."

"I'm fini, Charlie. How did it happen so fast to me?"

"You're not finished, Marge. *You* finished? I'd like to see the day. Right now you're drunk. You can see only the dark side. But you'll bounce, Marge. I know you will."

"I'm always drunk."

"That's not true."

"Don't tell me what's true. I lean on a liquid crutch. Can't walk with it; can't walk without it."

"Get a grip on yourself, Marge . . . Look, why don't I run back to the office and pick up my things, and then take you home?"

"Don't walk out on me, Charlie."

"I'm not going to. You wait for me. I have to call my wife and Bruce, and get my coat."

"You know what the night nurse at the hospital said?"

"Tell me when I come back."

"She said I had the body of a woman of thirty. She was bathing me and she said I had the body of a woman of thirty. I haven't even got stretch marks, papa-doodle."

"Will you wait right here?"

"I'm broke, papa-doodle."

"Well, you don't need any money. I'm signing the check."

"No, I mean I'm *broke*. My finances, as you say, are *not* in good shape, 'fact, after I pay Bonwit Teller what I owe them, I'll have $200 to my name."

"What?"

"And all my stocks are phffft—liquidated, papa-doodle."

"I thought you saved."

"I had to pay those ovary-robbers, papa-doodle."

"Did it take *everything?*"

"I didn't have that much."

"I can't believe it. Where did it go? You made a hell of a lot, Marge!"

"Phffft!"

"Listen, Marge, let me—"

"I'm really on the ash-heap, papa-doodle. I don't know why I just don't give up the ghost. Any normal woman would go out and slash her wrists."

"I *have* to stop in at the office, Marge," Charlie said. "Now, do you want to wait here? I'll take you home."

"No. Jest put me in a cab. I'm fini!"

"I'll put you in a cab, then," Charlie said. "And you go home and sack out. You'll feel better tomorrow."

"No, I won't."

"Yes, you will," Charlie said. "Waiter!"

Charlie guided her slowly through the lobby of the hotel.

"I'm a barren woman, boys," she called to two bell-boys who were standing near the door.

"There's Miss Weather," one murmured loud enough for Charlie to hear.

Out front, Charlie pressed a half-dollar into the doorman's hand.

"We need a cab in a hurry," he said.

Marge leaned against him. "Did you hear how I entertained them all at Continental Electric?" she said. " 'Sss very very funny . . . I sang."

"I didn't hear," Charlie said.

"I sang *Friggin In The Riggin,* papa-doodle. Wanta hear?"

"No," Charlie said. "Not now."

She sang it anyway.

Charlie said, "Shhh, Marge, please."

"I don't have any," she said.

"We'll get a cab in a minute," he said.

She lurched against him heavily. Her head fell on his shoulder and she kept singing the song. People passing snickered at them. The doorman stood in the street blowing his whistle frantically.

She was too drunk to make it on her own.

When the cab came, Charlie got in too.

It was ten minutes to five.

MARCH 6, 1957

CHAPTER SEVENTEEN

AT A quarter to five, Wally Keene got off the elevator on the twenty-first floor and walked up to Sandra Scott's desk, his lean face breaking into a grin when he saw her.

"Mr. Cadence will see you in a moment," she said.

"When did the prodigal return?"

She didn't answer him.

He stuck his hands in his flannel trousers and rocked on his heels, standing before her desk.

"We thought we were going to have to break in a new girl."

"We?" she said.

"Bruce and I."

She put a piece of paper into her typewriter, ignoring him.

"Come on, Miss Scott," he said. "I'm not a *real* sibling, you know."

"Sibling?" she said. "I'm afraid I don't understand, Mr. Keene."

"Well, in plain words, I'm not rivaling with you for

Bruce's favor. I'm not a threat, Miss Scott. He thinks a lot of you."

"What are you talking about?"

"You shouldn't let these inter-family relations traumatize you, Miss Scott."

She said, "I'm very busy."

"I'd like to be your friend. Is that plain enough? You and Bruce and I are all working on the same team, aren't we?"

"Mr. Keene," she said, "I don't know what you want, but I'm very busy."

"Did Charlie Gibson send up anything on the dummy?"

"There's the phone, Mr. Keene," she said. "Mr. Gibson's extension is Four-o-nine."

"Thanks, Miss Scott. I'll remember that. That's more or less what I wanted to know. Whether or not I could break down the defense mechanism . . . I see I can't."

Sandra Scott began to type.

"That's a very sick attitude, Miss Scott," Keene said, "and the sick get sicker . . . Like Marge Mann."

She kept on typing.

"Sometimes it pays to cooperate, even if you don't feel like it. I thought we might cooperate, but I guess you're too mixed up, Miss Scott."

The buzz of the intercom interrupted him.

She answered it; then she said, "Mr. Cadence will see you now, Mr. Keene."

"Thanks, Miss Scott," he said. "Thanks for everything. And lots of luck."

"Sorry to call you up at the close of the day like this, Wally, but—"

"Not at all, Bruce. What's the trouble?"

"I want to hold the dummy."

"Look, Bruce, the mock-up should go out to advertisers on the twelfth. That's less than a week away. We're playing it too damn close as it is."

"I know, I know. Sit down." He motioned to a chair

and sat down in his own. He bit the end off a cigar
and poked the tobacco with a stick. Wally leaned forward, flicking his lighter to a flame.

"Thanks . . . The way I feel, Wally, to be perfectly
frank, is that Charlie should have a chance to say how
he feels about the book."

"Then he *hasn't?*"

"He's been out all afternoon."

"Out!"

"I know, I know . . . I don't know where he is . . .
But Marge Mann never returned from lunch."

"Oooh. That's it."

"It could very well be. Bonnie said they had lunch
together though, and then Charlie came back to the
office. Shortly after he came back, he disappeared.
Didn't take his coat—just walked out. Didn't say where
he was going, and isn't back yet." Cadence glanced
at his watch. "Well, it's five to five."

"Bruce, the dummy should be at the printers' right
now. *You* know that."

"I phoned them. They can wait until six."

"It's pretty obvious, isn't it, that Charlie doesn't care
one way or the other? He's never been particularly
interested in it."

"He doesn't like it, doesn't like the idea of it."

"All right, we went into all of that. And we agreed
it was the only thing we could do under the circumstances to pull us out of the red."

"But *is* it, Wally?"

"Did Charlie come up with a better idea?"

Cadence puffed on his cigar thoughtfully.

Wally said, "Just because he doesn't like the idea,
doesn't mean he should ignore it. We decided on it,
didn't we? So it's policy, isn't it? Charlie knew it had
to be at the printers' today. He should have said something. He was required to."

"Yes, he should have said something . . . I keep
thinking he'll come through . . . I keep thinking that
maybe the reason for the delay—maybe even the reason

for his being gone all afternoon, has something to do with this problem . . . Maybe Charlie's at work on it."

"What's to be done on it, Bruce? All he has to do is okay it. Or criticize it. What else?"

"I know Charlie, I think." Cadence got up from his desk and walked to the window. "I keep wondering if he isn't perhaps on the track of something else . . . It's not like Charlie to be silent, the way he has been . . . about Marge—and now about this. I think it might be the calm before the storm."

"You mean you think he'll come up with another idea?"

Cadence said, "Maybe, Wally . . . maybe."

"It's a little late for that, isn't it?"

"I don't feel comfortable about the dummy, Wally."

"Bruce, that's obvious. But we've got to move *fast!* That dummy should go to the printers' immediately."

"We can afford a day's wait, I feel."

"I don't think we can."

"I'm sorry, Wally, but I think I'm going to insist on a hold until we hear from Charlie."

"You've got to cut the umbilical cord some day, Bruce. It's ridiculous to imagine that Charlie's going to come through at the last minute with a miraculous answer to our problems. Look, Bruce." Keene got up and walked over to the window by Cadence. "Charlie's probably out on a wing-ding with Marge Mann. I told you not to depend on Charlie today. He's in a tight situation. He's probably loaded down with guilt. I told you all of that."

"I've known Charlie a long time."

"If he really had any strong objections to the dummy, he would have voiced them by now."

"Maybe," Cadence said, "maybe not. Charlie's a funny guy."

"Has he read it?"

"Bonnie said he read it after lunch."

"Then it's obvious he doesn't care, Bruce. He knows

it has to be at the printers'. He would have said something."

"I don't think he would have okayed it, Wally."

"Then where are we?"

"Waiting for Charlie's reaction," Cadence answered. "And I just have a hunch it'll surprise us."

"That's sheer fantasy, Bruce. I don't mind telling you."

"We'll see," Cadence said. "I just wanted to tell you that I'm going to hold it."

He put his cigar in his ashtray on the desk and bent down to pick up his briefcase. He began stuffing it with papers from the desk.

Keene said, "I think you'll be sorry."

"Wait and see," Cadence answered. "I think I know Charlie."

Keene started for the door, then stopped. "I see Miss Scott came back."

"Yes, shortly after you left."

"I was just noticing her while I was waiting for you. She's certainly a case of nerves, isn't she?"

"Sandy?" Cadence looked surprised. "I didn't think she looked any different. She was just in here."

"Look closely," Keene said. "I noticed it right away. A bundle of nerves, poor kid . . . Probably needs a rest."

"Really?" Cadence said.

Keene was about to add more when the phone rang on Bruce's desk.

He waited as Bruce took the call, and heard him say, "Are you sure, Bonnie? . . . I see . . . You're *sure* . . . all right then, thank you."

Bruce Cadence put the phone back in its cradle.

He said solemnly, "Well, that's that, I guess."

"What's up?"

"Charlie just called Bonnie to say he wouldn't be back this afternoon," Cadence answered. "He told her to call me and tell me he okays the *Vile* dummy."

MARCH 6, 1957

CHAPTER EIGHTEEN

"DID YOU call Bruce?" she said.

"Yes," he said, "and now you better sack out."

In the bathroom, she had vomited. Charlie had heard the repeated flushings of the toilet as she had tried to cover up the sounds of her gagging. He had smoked a cigarette and stared at the saffron-colored cotton rug in her apartment. There were four or five overflowing ashtrays scattered about on tables; empty beer cans, glasses with an inch of melted ice cubes and stale Scotch at their bottoms; a crossword puzzle book with all the puzzles worked, a plate of crackers and cheese on the floor by the hide-a-bed; and next to it, a large bottle of Bromo-Seltzer, and a spoon.

She looked pale and old standing in the doorway. Her hair was mussed, her lipstick smeared. There were wet stains on the front of her navy blue silk blouse. But she was more sober; not completely sober, but better.

Charlie thought, I can leave her now.

She said, "Did you give Bruce hell about the dummy?"

"I didn't talk to him directly," Charlie said. "I put an okay on it . . . You better go to bed, Marge. Get some rest. It's been a rough day."

"Won't you have *one* drink with me, papa-doodle?"

"I don't want any more. I have to drive."

"Will you sit with me while I have just one, papa-doodle?"

"All right," Charlie said, "but you'll have to make it a quick one."

147

She went carefully into the kitchen, calling behind her, "You going to tuck me in, Charlie?"

"I can't stay that long, Marge."

"I'm going right to bed."

"I have to go in about eight minutes," he said.

"Remember how you used to like to watch me undress?"

"I remember."

"I'm going to undress for bed while I'm having my quick one," she said, coming back with the bottle.

She set it on the coffee table before the couch and sat down next to Charlie. He could smell the odor of vomit and mouth gargle.

He said, "Marge, I'll send some feelers out on a new job for you. I'll ask around."

"Sure," she said. "You do that, papa-doodle."

"You've got to pull yourself together and face this thing."

"I'm face to face with it, papa-doodle."

"*Seriously*, Marge."

"What am I supposed to do? Go around begging for a job?"

"No, but you should—"

"Charlie," she interrupted him, "why don't you stay over?"

"What?"

"Why don't you stay over tonight. We could go around the corner to The Gold Coin and have some dinner, and then we could come back and listen to records, maybe even read some poetry. Charlie, would you like that? It'd be like old times."

"You know better than that," he said.

"Don't leave me alone, Charlie. I don't want to be left alone tonight. I want to—recapture something. Something's lost."

"Marge, think about the future, not the past."

"The past was swell, Charlie, wasn't it? It was better than now."

"The past always improves, Marge," he said, reaching for another cigarette.

She took it from his hand.

"I'll do it. Remember how I used to always do this?"

"Uh-huh."

"Nothing's different, Charlie. I'm the same. Do you think I've changed? Tell me honestly." She lit the cigarette and handed it back to him, the tip of it wet from her mouth.

"Yes, you've changed. And I've changed. We're older."

"Physically I'm the same. 'Course," she laughed in a silly too-cry way, "I don't got my organs, but it don't *show*, papa-doodle. The night nurse at the hospital said I had the body of a woman of thirty. She was bathing me and she said I had the body of a woman of thirty."

Charlie said, "You told me."

"Did I?"

"This afternoon."

"You wanna watch me undress, Charlie? You always used to like to, remember." She got up and took a swig of the drink she had poured for herself.

Charlie said, "I really have to go."

"Just watch me undress," she said. "The way you used to like to. Remember? I stand right in the middle of the room." She weaved across the rug. "And take everything off."

"Don't, Marge," Charlie said. "Come back and finish your drink and then I have to leave. Come on, now. Come back and we'll have a cigarette, and then I'm going."

"First the blouse," she said, undoing the buttons, kicking off her heels. Then, "Oops," she said, "I forgot. You used to like it if I kept my heels on until toward the end." She stumbled to get into her heels, the blouse open.

When her feet were back in her shoes, she took off the blouse and stood in her bra, smiling at Charlie.

He sighed and sucked in on his cigarette. He could not look too long at her.

"Now the skirt drops," she said, "but first I want a little more of my drink." She walked over to the table, drank from the glass, and stood in front of Charlie.

"Want to unbutton the skirt, darling?"

His fingers fumbled with the button.

"All right," she said, "now help me like you like to do."

"Marge," he said—but he didn't know what more to say. His hands remained in his lap.

"Pull it down, Charlie. Don't you want to?"

"No, Marge. I'm going."

"Charlie, just wait until I'm in bed, please. Don't leave me alone until I'm in bed."

"You'll have to hurry," he told her. "Take your clothes off quickly and slip into bed. Go in the bathroom and get undressed."

"Don't you want to watch me, Charlie?" she whined. "Am I that repulsive?"

"Marge, please. I'm in a great hurry."

"Ping!" she said. "There goes the skirt."

She stepped out of it, wearing now the bra and the half slip as she stood by the couch.

"Want to unhook me, Charlie?"

She turned around with her back to him, and stooped a little.

Woodenly, Charlie undid the fasteners.

She turned around then, and tried to sit on Charlie's lap.

Charlie stood up. "Marge, why are you doing this? *Don't* do this."

His back was to her; he heard her moving behind him, undressing more, wordlessly. He stood there hating himself, feeling he could cry for her, wanting to get out. A depressive sickness was filling him with some sudden shame over some uncertain thing he must have done or left undone.

He could hear a clock ticking; the rustle of clothing; the clink of ice cubes in a glass; but he could not speak or turn around or go or move.

How long was it before eventually she said his his name.

"What?" he murmured.

Then, from behind, he felt her arms come around his body, and knew she was naked now. She repeated his name.

She said, "Turn to me, Charlie. Don't alienate me. Don't everybody alienate me!"

Gently he turned around, taking her hands from him, not looking at her body, but at her eyes. They were filled with tears.

He said quietly, "All right, Marge. How about bed? I'll get it down for you."

"Thank you, Charlie," she said. "You care what happens to me, don't you?"

"Yes," Charlie Gibson said.

He walked across the room and pulled out the hide-a-bed. He heard her pour more liquor from the bottle on the table into her glass.

When the bed was down, he said, "All right, Marge. Come on now. I'll tuck you in."

"Charlie?"

"What?"

"Turn around and look at me, Charlie. Please look at me."

Slowly, he turned and his eyes saw her.

Her body was very white. There were red marks where elastic had worn into the flesh, and her body sagged. And he suddenly noticed the scar of her appendix operation, which had always been there; and her body was a tired body; it was sad and spent and sixty.

"Do you know what the night nurse at the hospital said, Charlie?"

"Yes," he said, "you told me."

"I haven't changed, have I?" she said.

"No," Charlie said. He said, "Come on, Marge: Get into bed."

"Could *you* still love me, Charlie?"

"Please, Marge," He noticed tears beginning in her eyes. "I'm very late."

"*Could* you?"

"Marge—"

"Charlie, answer me. Could you still love me?"

"Yes," Charlie made himself say. "Yes. Your body is —very nice."

"Nice?"

"Yes." He looked down at the rug. She was simply standing there by the coffee table, looking at him.

"Not beautiful any more? I remember how your eyes got bright when you looked at me. Now you can't look at me, can you, papa-doodle?"

"I have to leave, Marge," he said helplessly. "I'll tuck you in if you'll come to bed now, but I *have* to leave.

"Don't leave me alone, papa-doodle. Not tonight. Stay over."

Charlie's fingers knotted to fists. He felt anger beginning in him, anger at all of it; and an immense and horrible pity for her, a shameful revulsion at her behavior, and a contempt for his own stumbling inadequacy.

"I'm begging you, Charlie," she said.

He looked at her. She was naked on her knees.

After he had helped her to her feet, she clung to him, sobbing.

"Help me, Charlie. I helped you once."

"I want to help you, but you won't let me. I will help you."

"Stay over," she begged. "Don't leave me alone tonight."

Charlie said, "Marge, I can't stay over."

"Make love to me. God, Charlie, I need love. I need love."

"No, Marge," he said, his tone more sharp than he intended it. "No."

Abruptly her mood changed.

She let go and walked to the coffee table. "Okay, papa-doodle," she said, "Okay. Margie'll just take her bottle and go where she's wanted." She began to walk away from the living room, into the bathroom. "To the medicine cabinet, Charlie. The chloral; the amytal; the Nembutal. Christ, have mercy on us. Freud, have mercy upon us. Life, have mercy upon us."

Charlie heard the door slam, then the bolt slipping into the lock.

At first, he had an impulse just to walk out of the apartment.

He stood and lit a cigarette, and heard the sound of the medicine cabinet banging shut.

He walked to the door of the bathroom.

"Marge," he said, "are you all right?"

She began to recite something. It was very familiar, a poem she had always liked. She recited it in a monotonous voice, like someone saying words from rote memory, statically:

"This is for those who work and those who may not,
For those who suddenly come to a locked door,
And the work falls out of their hands;
For those who step off the pavement into hell,
Having not observed the red light and the warning
    signals
Because they were busy or ignorant or proud—"

"Marge!" Charlie said, "I'm going to leave."

"This is for those who are bound in the paper chains
That are stronger than links of iron; this is for
    those—"

"Do you hear me, Marge?"

"Who each day heave the papier-mâché rock
Up the huge and burning hill,
And there is no rock and no hill, but they do not
    know it."

"Marge!" Charlie shouted. "Answer me. Are you all right?"

"This is for those who wait till six for the drink, .
Till eleven for the tablet;
And for those who cannot wait but go to the dark-
*   ness;*
And for those who long for the darkness but do
*   not go,*
Who walk to the window and see the body falling,
Hear the thud of air in the ears,
And then turn back to the room and sit down again,
None having observed the occurrence but them-
*   selves."*

"Good-by, Marge," Charlie shouted again.

"Good-by, Charlie," she answered. "I've taken the pills. It won't be long now . . .

> *Christ have mercy upon us,*
> *Freud have mercy upon us,*
> *Life have mercy upon us . . ."*

MARCH 6, 1957

CHAPTER NINETEEN

AFTER THE phone call, Joan Gibson returned to the living room.

She said to the guests, "It was Charlie."

Aileen Tullett said, "Is he all right?"

"Naturally, naturally . . . Just tied up."

"Aw, honey, he *forgot!*"

"Never mind," Charlie Gibson's wife said, "we may as well eat."

Roger Tullett knocked the dottle out of his pipe and chuckled, "Another executive business crisis, I'll bet!"

"Oh, sure," she said. "Sure . . . that's why Bonnie knew all about it when I called her."

"Well, didn't he *say* where he was?" Aileen asked.

"He said he'd explain later . . . anyone for chicken tetrazzini? And birthday cake?"

Bob Carroll stood up. "Now, now, Joanie, don't let this thing get you. Charlie probably has a perfectly logical explanation."

Joan Gibson said, "Or a perfectly logical excuse . . . Well, come on, let's start the party rolling,"

The doctor was dog-tired.

Before he had been called here, he had operated on a cancer case, found it had spread hopelessly, knew the woman would die. Young woman, in her ninth month of pregnancy.

He was out of patience with the man.

Gibson his name?

Gibson kept repeating himself: "She was reciting poetry and—"

"These types always recite poetry," the doctor said. "Usually dreary, self-pitying poetry. They know them all."

"She'll pull through, won't she?"

"Just needs her stomach pumped out."

"Shouldn't we try to revive her and walk her around the room or something?"

"She's had too much to drink. These types always do it this way."

"I should have told her I'd stay with her. She's really been through the mill."

"She didn't take many," the doctor said. "Her prescription wasn't that big. It's more liquor than anything else. These types never take enough."

"What do you mean by that?" Gibson looked angry.

The doctor said, "Alert the elevator man that the ambulance is coming . . . You sure she has no one to stay here with her?"

"No, no one."

"What about you?"

"I can't," Gibson said, "I—"

"Then she'll have to go to the hospital," the doctor answered curtly. "Get the elevator man."

After the man left the apartment, the doctor walked over to the hide-a-bed and took the woman's pulse. He noticed the unkempt look of the apartment, the beer cans, ashtrays, liquor bottles. He thought to himself tiredly that it was one of these boringly typical suicide attempts: the aura of the orgy; the "Mr. Gibson" who obviously belonged elsewhere—with his family—the nakedness; the pulled-down hide-a-bed; the time and trouble everyone would have to go to—doctors and nurses who could be concerned with more serious matters; the stubborn selfishness of such cases—sleeping-pill swallowers who always remember to phone, before, or have someone around to rescue them, infantile people who purposely inflict injury on themselves to force others' attentions. It was so unnecessary, he thought wearily, and so usual. Routine in this city; every night a few.

Mr. Gibson reappeared, began pacing the room.

The doctor said, "You'll accompany her to the hospital, will you not."

"Yes. Yes, I will."

"How many times has she tried this before?"

"What? . . . Look, doctor, this isn't just dramatics. This woman's been through the mill. She's not one of these—"

"I know," the doctor sighed, "she's *different*."

"Are you scared?" the boy asked the girl, taking her arm as they went up the steps.

"A little." Then she said, "No, Dud, I'm more than a little scared. I'm petrified!"

"I'll be with you. I'll be right at your side."

"I know that. It's just—it's so embarrassing."

"But it's the only way. We agreed on that, Janie."

"Yes, we agreed on that."

"Okay," he said. "We might as well go on in and get it over with."

He had gone into the bar while he was taking his walk, shortly after he'd finished his rewrite. Mitzie had been dozing on the bed in the hotel room, and he hadn't bothered to awaken her. He'd folded his manuscript and put it in the inside pocket of his overcoat. Then he'd left the hotel and headed uptown, crossing over to Broadway.

He had ordered two drinks and he was on his third, standing there with the manuscript in his hand, half reading it, half watching what was going on around him. It made him sick and at the same time it fascinated him, and repulsed him—the way a snake would—this bar. He'd been in a dozen or more just like it since he'd come to New York, and each time he left one he swore it was the last one. And every time he came back, whenever he could, at the slightest opportunity.

In St. Louis he would never think of frequenting such a bar, even though he knew where every one of them was. Knew, and often walked by them, peered in, and went on. Sometimes he told himself the reason he had the list of these bars in his wallet was that one day he was going to do an exposé of them. It was a good idea; it would sell papers. They deserved it, anyway. God damn them, he would tell himself, and his fists would clench in the pockets of his trench coat, and he would think as he always did of his Mikie, his son—this was before Mike was killed—and he would think, What if some goddam faggot ever got his filthy hands on my boy, what if *that* happened? Why, God, he'd kill him, lousy faggot; kill him if anyone ever got his hands on Mike.

Then he'd remember Otto Avery and always he would weep inside himself, and wonder at the irony of it—at Avery taking the boy *he* was and molesting it, and at Avery giving back the boy Mikie was.

It never occurred to Basescu that Mike could be taken.

When it happened, it seemed again somehow to be reaching out to destroy again. And he blamed Avery.

It was Avery's fault; not any Kismet, nor war, but Avery's—He blamed for it, and people like him.

For his own part in what had happened between himself and Avery those years and years past, Basescu had litt.: memory. He would not picture it in his mind; he would only picture Avery and think of himself, God, I was such a kid. Such a kid—and Avery ruined me.

It was incongruous that he thought with satisfaction that he had shouldered a responsibility Avery had shunned, that he had married Mitzie, and raised Mike. Yet he never thought of Mike as belonging to Avery. Mike was simply what Avery had robbed him of—a boy—a healthy young boy. His—Basescu's—boy.

That night as Basescu stood in the bar watching and listening to the swish voices around him, he felt a victory—not a victory over these she-males, but rather a victory with them over Avery. He imagined his story screaming Avery's guilt at the public from the pages of the exposé magazine; and somehow those sweet-smiling, vulnerable, and fading faces around him seemed his accomplices, for some Avery had victimized too, Basescu felt, and his revenge was theirs as well.

He ordered another drink, and as he was raising it to his lips in an unspoken toast to his unwitting colleagues, someone spoke to him.

Basescu turned.

The man was tall, muscular and handsome, around thirty-five, well-spoken.

Basescu said, "What did you say?"

"Just hello," the man said.

"How do you do."

The man said, "Busy in here tonight."

"I wouldn't know. I just stopped in here for a drink. I've never been here before."

"Nor I," the man said.

Basescu was uneasy. He felt somehow that he should explain to the man that it was only an accident that he was drinking in this bar.

"I'm quite surprised at this place," Basescu said.

The man chuckled. "Oh, well—"

"I didn't know the kind of place it was."

"Poor guys," the man said. He shrugged, smiling.

Basescu liked him. He made Basescu feel more assured.

Basescu said, "Yes, they're not responsible. Someone did it to them, I suppose."

"Yes."

"It's a pity."

"They seem happy."

"Yes, don't they. Yes, they do seem happy."

"Sure, they're having a good time."

"I guess you're right."

"Only deadheads like us can't enjoy ourselves."

Basescu laughed enthusiastically. He felt somehow oddly relieved.

"Yes," he said. "Yes."

"You going to have another here?" the man asked. "Or do you want to go along?"

"Well, I don't know," Basescu said. He thought of the money he had left in his wallet. Not enough for a lot of drinking, that was sure, but he was going to allow himself to have one more when the man said, "How about a walk?"

"All right. Good!"

It was strange that Basescu did not give it a second thought. He had a wild feeling of undeniable ease with this man, a sudden wild feeling of absolute familiarity with him, as though he had known him before. He gathered up his change and repeated, "All right. Good!"

The man followed behind him.

Basescu heard someone on the way out say to him, "Hey, Mary, it's the first of the month."

He flushed, hating the way he had been addressed; not understanding it, but embarrassed by it.

He said to the man outside, "They just call out whatever they feel like to strangers."

The man smiled. "Yeah," he said. "Where to?"

"I don't care," Basescu said.

"I'd sort of like to sit down. How about you?"

"Well," Basescu said, remembering the unkempt look of the lobby of his hotel, "I don't know— We could get coffee, I suppose."

"That's not very comfortable."

"All right," Basescu said. "My hotel is nearby. We could go there. It's not much, but—"

The man smiled again. "All right," he said, "but I want to lock my car. Come on."

Basescu followed the man. As he did, he wondered what on earth he was doing, going along with a stranger he had never met before in his life. And yet, what was there so familiar about this man? Why was he, Basescu, who rarely made friends—indeed, *never* did— so completely at ease with this one?

He thought of being mugged, but it was preposterous. They were right out on Broadway, in plain sight.

As they came to the curb, the man turned to Basescu. He said, "Sorry, I have to give you bracelets now."

"What?" Basescu smiled, not understanding the joke.

"Put your arms up," he said.

Then Basescu saw two things—handcuffs and a police officer's badge.

"W-why?" Basescu stammered.

The man said, "Come and hear a fairy tale, for one thing."

The phrase came slowly to Basescu's mind. It was the lead on his story about Otto. No, it was the title. The man must have looked down on the bar and seen the title page of Basescu's manuscript.

It read: COME AND HEAR A FAIRY TALE.

Basescu said, "Wait a minute—you're making a mistake—" He began to feel his pockets for his manuscript.

"Don't any of you guys ever get pinched without that old refrain?" The man snapped the handcuffs around Basescu's wrists. "Come on. My partner's parked, waiting."

"I can explain this," Basescu protested. "Where's my manuscript?"

"I got the piece of paper, buddy."

"There were ten pieces of paper!"

"I got the one *we* want, mister . . . Got to hand it to you, a very unique approach."

Basescu tried to say more, but the man pushed him into the back seat of the police car.

He found two other men there beside him, a lisping older one who was comforting a slim, blond boy who was crying.

The officer in the front seat moved over for the man who got behind the wheel.

As the motor started, the older man said, "Listen, you shouldn't arrest her. She's very respectable. She's a male nurse!"

"Sure, she is, Mabel," the man said. "And we're all on our way to Niagara Falls. This is your honeymoon."

Basescu's cheeks burned.

He said, "Won't you listen to me! Won't you give me a chance to explain! I just wandered into that bar! I didn't even know—"

"Come and hear my fairy tale," the man said, swinging the car out into traffic.

"Listen to me, please!" Basescu said.

The older man said, "They never listen at the first of the month, Mary. Their quotas, you know, Mary. No one to arrest but the girls."

The blond boy began to sob audibly.

"It's all right, honey," the older man said. "They'll let you off. It's your first offense."

"Sure," the man said as they headed downtown, "and besides, she's very respectable. She's a male nurse."

Then, when the policeman laughed, Basescu heard the sound of other laughter from years and years past, and unconsciously, trancelike, his clenched fist unrolled, and he held his palm open for the money he would not receive this time.

Wally Keene liked the feeling of success, and though in his own mind he was—as he thought of it—"on the middle rung working up," he was acquainted with the feeling, adjusted, he believed, to its inevitability—for he had, not always, but certainly more often than not, gotten what he set out to get.

As a boy, he had vied with his brothers—three of them—for his father's favor. He had vied and been rewarded, and he could still remember how, as a not completely innocent four-year-old, he had won the highest praise from adults gathered in the family's parlor, their charmed and captivated laughter at his remark: "Sometimes I wish the Keenes had only *one* boy, and that he was I." He could remember the almost worshipful sparkle to his father's eye amidst the laughter, as son and father regarded one another then. And it seemed the elder Keene in that moment promised Wally that so it would be, if not in reality, in his heart; and so it was.

Yet the boy had worked for that reward. He had, with the instinctive determination which he seemed to possess even then, found ways to woo his father away from the other three, memorized the cunningness that pleased his father, and sought to imitate it and dress it anew before presenting it. He knew somehow, with the deceivingly sly ingenuousness of a child, that a big word won approval, that demonstrativeness won approval (so that he alone among the four boys was called the affectionate one, the way he ran always to his father and kissed and hugged the man, waiting for the, "There now, that's daddy's boy," while he thought, My brothers aren't—*I* am) and knew, too, how to provoke his mother so terribly that in a fit of temper she would reprimand him severely, and he would have a wound to show his father, who was adamantly opposed to physical punishment for the children.

As a boy, he knew success and its feeling, both at home and later in prep school.

It was easy for him to say things quite frankly, because the things he said he did not necessarily mean. He said them for their effect. So that he could walk up to another lad quite confidently and allow: "You know, you have a damn nice pitching arm. I think you'll go places," or "Good comment in Lit this morning, Bill. You're a brain. I envy you," (said to a duller student than he was) or "You're more mature than most around here," (said to some bullheaded nitwit) until eventually, through his outspokenness and his self-confidence (he never let it seem to be the cocky kind, but tempered it with a faint suggestion of humility), he gained the stature of mediator, counselor, non-academic philosopher. In short, leader.

College found him accepted in the best clubs, dating the most beautiful girls, and having the good sense in his senior year to become engaged to one who was not as beautiful as she was potentially valuable. Susan Keene's father had the best kind of wealth, the inherited kind, and though he was Spartan enough in temperament to admire anyone who started "from the bottom," he was not at all averse to financing a son-in-law who could prove he more appropriately deserved the milieu at the top.

Wally Keene liked the feeling of success and he counted on it, counted on a rapid rise within Cadence, which would ultimately take him beyond his present goal—Charlie Gibson's position—on to complete control of the Cadence Corporation.

In his daydreams, there was the speech: "Look, Bruce, no reason at all why you can't stay on. Hell, we want you to stay on!"

Yet while he dreamed this dream, Wally Keene did not sit back and taste success not yet accorded him. Instead he planned, planned everything. Even his psychoanalysis was part of that plan.

"It's better to get the kinks out now," he would tell Susan.

And Susan would say, "But what *are* the kinks, Wally?"

"Everyone has kinks," would be his answer—fortified with the offense, "Don't pretend!"

And just as he had planned it, the retort would shut her up.

Susan was convinced that her husband, since he had entered analysis, knew everything she was thinking.

To Susan's mind, something which had happened one afternoon on a Madison Avenue bus symbolized everything about her husband and his psychoanalysis.

They had been jerking along the avenue in the front of the bus, and the driver, a fearfully gruff and rude fellow, had been snapping at all the passengers. When the bus reached Fortieth Street, where the Keenes were going, Wally and Susan attempted to get off the bus at the front, just as new fares attempted to get on.

The driver turned and bellowed at Wally: "You stupid ass! You a hick or something? Get off ina back! You shouldn't be on buses, you dope!"

Susan was horribly embarrassed. Everyone was staring at them. She always became embarrassed and humiliated under such circumstances, even though it was not her fault, and that afternoon she was doubly mortified because it had happened to her husband. Publicly, she felt, he had been made a fool of; called "stupid" by a bus driver.

But Wally, poised before the resultant laughter and smirks of all beholding their situation, quite calmly led Susan to the rear, remarking in a mild tone to all who listened—in a mild, sincere, and quite serious tone, "That man is very sick."

When she thought about it, Susan believed that Wally had reacted almost like Bernard Baruch would have, or Nehru, Gary Moore, or Norman Vincent Peale. And she knew that Wally's psychoanalysis had done that, and she hung on to his arm proudly, as though she were walking with Bernard Baruch, or Gary Moore or Norman Vincent Peale. Somehow she had reservations about walking with Nehru.

She had even sent it into *The Saturday Evening Post's* "Perfect Squelch" column, but nothing had come of it. Only an acknowledgment.

That evening of 6 March, Susan Keene felt even more in awe of "this psycho thing," as she had come to phrase it in her mind.

She and Wally were having their coffee in the living room of their modest ranch home, seated around the coffee table, which was an antique, and had once been a cobbler's bench.

Wally had his tie undone, and it was hanging around his collar.

She was fingering it affectionately as he talked, fingering it and thinking how clever he was, and wondering vaguely if he thought *she* needed psychoanalysis. He had never mentioned it.

". . . so you see," Wally was saying, "you need more than a good record business-wise. Sure, Cadence knows I'm on the ball business-wise. If he never knew it before, he knew it today. I mean, *after all*, Charlie just—"

"You've got a spot on your tie, honey."

"I took the trouble to stop in at the library and look Bruce up. You know he's in Who's Who In America too. Not just New York. You can learn a lot about a man, looking him up. Golf, for example. He's a golfer. I'm going to bone up on my golf. Wouldn't do any harm for us to join a club. *His* club. Your dad can help us out there."

"Daddy used to recite a poem about golf," she said. "See if I can remember it. Umm. I know:

> *The golf links lie so near the mill*
> *That almost every day*
> *The laboring children can look out*
> *And watch the men at play.*"

Wally shot her an angry look. "Oh for Chrissake!" he said.

"Well, it isn't *my* poem, darling."

"It's just like him! Archaic and sentimental! The mill children, f'Chrissake!"

"What else did you find out?"

"Quit pulling at my tie . . . His favorite charity is The Lighthouse. Wouldn't hurt you to take a couple afternoons off and read to the blind."

"And hire someone for Billy and Alice? That's not in our budget."

"Well, it'll *be* in our budget. Honey, I'm shooting for long-range things. Now, I think I've got Cadence on my performance business-wise, but now we go beyond that. That's where Charlie Gibson missed out. He never realized that in the business world you're a whole man, not just a nine-to-five man, and you've got to sell yourself right down the line. You've got to make yourself over, if necessary. You've got to take into consideration the psychological factors. Figure your top man out, and then shoot for him. Quit pulling at my tie, Susan!"

"Do you think I need analysis?"

"Oh, Christ!"

"What's the matter?"

"I'm trying to tell you something and you interrupt me!"

"I'm sorry, dear."

"You do it purposely. You can't stand any competition!"

"I'm *sorry*, dear."

"And fingering my tie is your way of overcoming that competition. The old female resort."

"It has a spot on it."

He said sarcastically, "*Sure*, it does!"

"Well, it does. Look!"

"In blunt words," Wally Keene said, "I'm too tired tonight."

She stared at him, not understanding for a moment. Then she said, "Is that what I meant?"

"That's what you meant, baby," he answered.

Often, since his analysis, situations like this had come up, in which he convinced her of some ulterior motive she was unaware of. It amazed her, even when she could not quite accept it. It fascinated her.

"Really?"

"Really!"

"I suppose I'm like that awful Marge Mann. Am I?"

"Never mind," he said impatiently, adding, "I fired her today . . . Now, where was I anyway—"

"She's fired, Wally?"

"That's right. That's one of the things I'm teaching Bruce. To clear out the weeds so the grass can grow. Another weed is Charlie Gibson, and that's what I'm getting at now. Bruce is so goddam sentimental. He won't let Gibson go because he's sentimental about the guy. That's all there is to it. Well, Gibson has got years and years of association with Bruce in his favor. I haven't! So I've got to make up for lost time, sort of get the wheels in motion for a transference, to use a psychological term. That's why—"

"How did she take it?" Susan asked.

Wally Keene tossed the pencil he was holding in his hand to the table. "Damn, God damn!" he shouted.

"W-what?" she said, startled.

"I'm sick of sentimental mish-mosh!" he said. "I'm sick of every woman in the world identifying with that C-cup bitch! I'm sick of everyone thinking I'm some kind of goddam monster! I'm sick and tired of it!"

"I didn't say—"

"Listen," Keene said, "I'm on my way up and I'm going to get there! A lot of guys in my game are like the hunchback girl in the old story. She met her boyfriend in the park one night and he didn't feel like making love. 'But you've got to,' she told him. 'I've already dug the hole.'"

Susan giggled at that, but Wally went on.

"Listen," he said, "a lot of guys in my game think because they've been in the business since the year one, and they fit in a certain slot, that slot'll always be theirs. They think small; they think narrow; they get fat; they get accustomed. Not me! I think big! My dad used to tell me that the day I could name the sum of money I'd be satisfied with for an annual salary, I'd be dead as a businessman. He was right! I don't know my limitations. I don't have any! I'm on fire. But listen to me, there are other guys on fire—not the hunchbacks like Charlie Gibson, but the others—the ones I have to outsmart at the top. Have to and *will!* Will because I'm not going to be afraid to get rid of people in my way! A giant can't walk without stepping on some ants!"

Susan Keene smiled. "Look out, all ants," she said, "there's a giant in our house." She was very proud of him.

Wally settled back on the couch, stretching his legs before him, his hands behind his head. "That's right! Look out ants!" he murmured.

MARCH 6, 1957

CHAPTER TWENTY

DRIVING ALONG Merritt Parkway that evening, Bruce Cadence remembered a conversation he had had with Barton Townsend, the mustard tycoon, down in the locker room at the club a couple of weeks ago.

Townsend had stood there in his lime-shaded silk shorts, sucking on an Uppman and splashing 4711 across his bare shoulders, shouting above the hissing of showers behind them: "Hell, Bruce, I don't give a hoot in hell *what* the differences are between the publishing game and the food game, personnel problems are the same anywhere. Business is just beginning to grasp this, just beginning, bigod, to realize that a hell of a lot that's wrong with the way things are going can be traced right back to a basic personnel problem. God sake, I can remember when I hired the production manager for my plant—just hired him; didn't give a damn if he was married, what his wife was like, what the hell kind of American he was, where the hell he went to school; just went and hired him—bang—like that. Just hired him because he seemed to have all the goddamn qualifications."

"I still hire men that way," Bruce said.

Townsend had wagged a fat finger at Bruce's nose and grunted, " 'At's just your mistake, mister. This day and age a man's got to know everything about the fellow he's asking to play on the team. And not just *that* either, God sake, a man's got to keep on the qui vive about the men he already has playing on his team, got to know the score. Maybe fellow in outfield worried about a goddam neurotic daughter, something. Maybe pitcher's got trouble with the other woman, God sake. Left field needs new car, right field wants to get his boy in Princeton, something . . . Man's got to keep on the qui vive about them all. 'At's the modern way. 'At's the new look in the world of business. The streamline trim, Bruce. You oughtta know that by now, God sake, Bruce. What the hell kind of penny-ante organization you running?"

Bruce Cadence remembered that he had sloughed it off as simply more routine locker-room palaver, the kind of palaver certain executive types reiterated endlessly, and which Bruce himself reacted to with faint amusement, striped with slight boredom. It was the kind of palaver Mildred always called "cigar smoke" whenever she heard their guests start such discussions. Yet seldom was there "cigar smoke" in the Cadence house, for neither were very enthusiastic entertainers. For the most part, they entertained only when they had to—relatives, or on rare occasions, couples from the club with whom they were able to have moderate and pleasant rapport, or the few time-tested "old friends" they had always known and seen at infrequent intervals.

The thought of entertaining business associates irritated Bruce Cadence. He believed—and he had always believed it—that when he left Cadence at five in the afternoon, that world was behind him. He had no interest in reviving it until nine the following morning.

Charlie Gibson seemed to feel the same way. It was one of the traits Bruce admired in Charlie. He remembered what Charlie used to say about the people who left the office with work crammed in their briefcases, and manuscripts under their arms.

Charlie used to say: "They couldn't have done much during the day if they have to do homework."

When Bruce tried to think back and remember how many times he and Charlie had met outside the office, he was unable to recall any other instances than the annual Cadence outings, in the summers, up in Greenwich, when all Cadence employees got together on the golf links, in the pool, on the lawns and terraces and dance floor of the club. He had never met Charlie's wife, and Charlie had never met Mildred. They had never had a drink together, and the only times they had had luncheon dates with one another were those times when it was necessary for a group of the executives at Cadence to meet with men from sales, circulation or advertising.

Bruce had always believed his and Charlie's association was just about the most perfect business relationship he could ask for. It was the way both seemed to want it.

Keene was not like that. From the moment Bruce had hired him, Sandy's buzzer had rung persistently to announce that Keene was on the wire, eager to pin Bruce down for a luncheon date. When finally Bruce gave in to Wally's persistence, and they faced one another across the table at The Blue Ribbon, Wally announced: "Now, absolutely no shop talk. Agreed?"

Warily, Bruce nodded; then watched Keene produce a pencil and a piece of paper from his pocket.

Keene said, "Draw a house," and passed the paper to Bruce.

"What for?"

"Just do it," Wally said. "It's a little psychology. It'll interest you."

"Why a house?"

"Just draw a house," Keene insisted. "You'll see."

Somehow Cadence suffered through the lunch without showing visible signs of his annoyance. He sat munching the German pancakes tiredly while Keene speared Bratwurst with one hand and held the picture of Bruce's house with the other, advising Bruce that the lack of a chimney on the house showed a lack of warmth in Bruce's early childhood; that the lack of a doorknob indicated a feeling of rejection; that the wide picture windows proved a tendency ("probably latent") for exhibitionism; and on and on, until Bruce's appetite was decimated, and his eagerness to finish the luncheon as quickly as possible so intense that he passed up coffee and dessert and mumbled some feeble excuse about a long-distance call back at the office.

"Some day," Wally had concluded the fiasco with these words, "we'll have to have a long talk about all these things you've revealed here, eh, Bruce?"

"I'm not very good at games," Bruce had answered.

"Oh, it's not a game," Wally Keene had protested. And Bruce Cadence was horrified to perceive that Keene was quite serious.

Even though Keene was more a maverick than anything else, Cadence kept the example of that luncheon front and center in his mind as concrete evidence that he had been right all along about not wishing to fraternize with his business associates.

Because occasionally, Bruce Cadence wondered if he were wrong to stay aloof. He wondered—and he and Mildred had discussed it more than often—if it were a serious flaw in him, not simply as a businessman, but as a personality.

One of the times he had pondered this was when Charlie was under the spell of Marge Mann, back in the early days of Charlie's association with Cadence, when the rumors finally and inevitably rose to the top, like all warm air; and Bruce first heard of their affair. There were months then when Charlie was not himself, times when he seemed irritable and depressed—and other times when his euphoria kept him from working well. Cadence thought of talking with him; thought of asking him up to his office and saying something like, "Sit down, Charlie. Let's have a chat . . ." But after that, what? What would he say after that? He realized Charlie and he had never once spoken of anything as personal as romantic interests. The likelihood that they ever would seemed somehow ludicrous.

So he had merely worried that he ought to do more; and then, suddenly, one morning it had passed. The affair had not been terminated, but Charlie had come to grips with it. Charlie was himself again, the crisis was averted.

Then Bruce prided himself on following the course most natural to Bruce Cadence, and upon handling the matter as he had felt he should. Or, in fact, not handling it at all. It was Charlie's to handle, and so it should be, Bruce believed. Should always be a man's own business.

As he drove, remembering Townsend's words and the recollections those words had invited, Cadence was more genuinely concerned about his world of business than he could ever remember being. Somehow what Townsend had said about a man "knowing everything about the fellow on his team" (even though Bruce was revolted by the way Townsend expressed himself) bothered Bruce, partly because he did not want to believe what he almost had to believe, that *this time* whatever it was with Charlie Gibson was *not* going to pass; and partly because Bruce Cadence wondered if he could have done anything, or said anything to Charlie, to prevent what now seemed inevitable—Bruce's firing Charlie. Not tomorrow, not next week—but soon, Bruce knew, he would be obliged—forced, really—to ask Charlie Gibson for his resignation.

He knew that was true, that it had to be so if he were to put Cadence Publications back on its feet, that he needed a more mature man than Wally Keene to temper Wally's ideas, and that he needed a man like the old Charlie to direct Cadence, with the same stubborn fire Charlie had had. And he knew too that it would have to be done quickly, and that once he set the wheels in motion, once he told Charlie of this decision, he would be able to find such a man. They were not that rare, nor that unobtainable. Bruce might not find "a nice guy" like Charlie. He might, as in the case of Keene, really dislike Charlie's replacement; still he could no longer afford to be sentimental. Cadence Publications could not afford it.

Somewhere in the back of his mind, he tried to frame with words what he would say to Charlie, how he would tell him, and yet before any one sentence could actually crystallize, he found himself in the same position he had been in during the afternoon with Keene in his office: saying, "I keep thinking Charlie will come through. I've known Charlie a long time."

And seeing, in his mind's eye, Wally Keene's smirk; hearing him remark wryly: "You've got to cut the umbilical cord some day."

Bruce began to believe for the first time that Wally Keene was right, that perhaps even Townsend was right—that all the streamliners and ballplayers and psychologists who had invaded the business world of nine-to-five-and-two-hours-out-for-lunch were right. Bruce Cadence was wrong, out-of-date, archaic. For now there was Freud, the Father; Gimmick, the Son; and Push, The Holy Ghost. *This* was the Trinity.

CHAPTER TWENTY-ONE

AT TWO in the morning, Charlie Gibson slipped the key in the lock and fumbled for the light switch.

The house was dark, silent. She had not left the porch light on for him. Warning enough. It made Charlie alternately angry and self-pitying to know that this reaction on Joan's part was one upon which he could always count, that at the slightest provocation (those were the words he chose in his mind—the slightest provocation) she would shut him out from herself. All the thoughts that had come to him upon similar occasions came to him again as he felt the wall for the light button: that he had married badly, that while his marriage, he supposed with the sighing attitude of tired resignation, was average—indeed, typical—it needn't have been so had he found a less selfish woman. A more selfless woman, one who lived for her man, catered to his moods and needs, understood him. Always when anything went wrong, any *little thing*, Charlie thought sadly, she withdrew from him. Was that what a wife was for? She had simply gone to bed and left him to stumble about blindly, turned the lights out in his own home—and who the hell paid the electric bills? Who had built this dark house, in the name of God? Was it hers or his? It wasn't *theirs*. She had turned the lights out and gone to bed!

Still he called, "Joan?"

He slapped his hat to the chair and stood looking at the sampler on the wall of the entranceway.

> *Home's not merely four square walls,*
> *Though with pictures hung and gilded;*

174

Home is where Affection calls,
Filled with shrines the Heart hath builded

He said, "What a laugh!" tripped on the edge of the umbrella stand, cussed and went toward the staircase. On his way up the stairs he noticed the pictures hung there, the framed family photographs: Joan and he posing behind two cardboard donkeys at Coney Island; Janie's first tooth; Joan and Janie and he on a picnic at Riis Park; Janie's first day at school—Trite goddam garbage, he thought, years of monotony adding up to nothing. What the hell!

He decided that when he went into the bedroom he would switch on the overhead light and play the radio, take his goddam time getting undressed, and not answer Joan. But when he got there, neither bed was occupied.

"Jesus!" Charlie muttered. "If this one of her—"

He went down the hall to the guest room. The door was shut, and when he tried the knob, it did not give.

Whose goddam guest room in whose goddam castle was it?

Tomorrow he decided he would ask for a divorce. Janie was running off with some drugstore cowboy and there was absolutely no rapport any more between himself and Joan. Why hang on to something pointless and meaningless? He would simply say, "Joan, I've thought it all out . . ."

"Joan?" he called.

He waited, almost savoring the knowledge that she would not answer him; more proof. He was glad she hadn't answered him—it would make it easier for him the next morning, when he would announce his decision after breakfast.

He said, "Did you ever remember my mentioning a woman named Marge Mann?" Paused, imagining her raising her head from the pillow, attentive now, alert. His voice grew. "She tried to kill herself tonight. . . . Did you hear me? . . . She tried to kill herself!"

He knew she heard him.

This time he shouted, "I had to fire her today."

And again, Charlie shouted—louder, "I've been through hell!"

There was silence.

"And I'm going to pour myself a drink!" he bellowed, "a good stiff goddam drink, because I've been through hell!"

Angrily he stormed down the hall, the stairs, past the family album hung there as though to shout the mediocrity of his existence, and he went into the living room.

The bourbon in the cabinet was a brand he did not like, a brand Joan knew he did not like, and as he poured himself a double shot he felt martyred and abused. He wandered around the living room aimlessly, picking fault with everything in it—the splotchy flowered slipcovers (Christ, Joan had every goddam color in the rainbow jammed into four walls) and there was still no footstool before his chair. For years he had wanted a footstool, a simple goddam want—a footstool —but he didn't even have a footstool; he had to put his feet up on the coffee table and she always said he was ruining the finish and he told her he wanted a footstool. Christ, he had begged her for a footstool, but there wasn't any, wasn't any. *"Home's not merely four square walls."* He could have been in a goddam accident for all she knew, and she was up there with her hair put up in pins, lollygogging around in the guest bed with Max Factor on her face, not giving a goddam.

Then on the triangular end table by his reading chair, where there was no footstool, he saw a package—birthday-wrapped.

He had forgotten about his birthday, forgotten that Joan had asked the Carrolls and the Tullets, and as he opened the box, fumbling with the ribbon, he remembered how he had cut her off over the telephone

when she had started to say, ". . . but the guests are
here and—"

He had snapped, "Tell me later!"

But Charlie, though he remembered this, thought:
Even does this to me on my birthday; and thought:
Gives me a gift I can't even open, ties the ribbons in
knots.

He had called Joan while he was waiting for the
doctor, after he had broken the bathroom door in with
the help of the elevator man. (The man had said, "This
is a wild one, all right," and Charlie had had a wretched
reaction. He had retorted, "Is she?" as though he were
surprised, as though he hardly knew Marge.) And
Marge was lying across from him when he called Joan,
like something dead under a sheet.

Charlie remembered that he had had the cruel, impulsive thought at that moment: Well, I hope she is—
one of those uncontrollable thoughts that a man is
ashamed of thinking, one that made mockery of his
concern, his pity. And Joan's voice had come through
the phone, "Later I won't be interested in your story!"

"Good!" he had said emphatically, thinking, No, I
don't want Marge to be dead.

From the gift-wrapped box, after he had labored with
the knotted pink and green ribbons, he lifted the shoes.
The taps were on the toes and heels.

Charlie looked at them blankly and put them back.
He drank his bourbon, standing there, suddenly aware
that he was fifty, aware perhaps for the first time that
he had lived half a century.

For some reason he thought of the words Marge had
recited through the bathroom door:

> *Christ have mercy upon us,*
> *Freud have mercy upon us,*
> *Life have mercy upon us.*

And he wondered why it was that suddenly the words
no longer sounded tragic and sad; but silly, dreary,

and sophomoric. And he poured himself more of the bourbon of the brand he did not like and Joan knew he did not like; and Charlie sank onto the couch.

When he reached for a cigarette in his pocket, his hand touched the letter Janie had sent him. Charlie took it out and began to reread it.

". . . guess I'm not very much like either you or mother . . ."

Was that true? Charlie didn't know; what *was* she like?

He remembered an afternoon when she was still in high school, when he had gone into the village for groceries, and Janie had asked him to pick up a particular brand and color of nail polish. Charlie had forgotten both the brand and the color, but he had bought polish at the drugstore.

She had held it in the palm of her hand, regarding it with slight disdain. "I wouldn't use this brand," she had said, "and only a perfect goon-girl would use this color. Honestly, Daddy!"

He remembered that he had thought it was curious and surprising that she had definite ideas about make-up, though he was not even sure why he had found it so peculiar. But he remembered that he had just stood there and wondered why he had never know that before about Janie, and he had clumsily tried to shut her palm around the bottle of polish, as though to wipe out the fact, and he had said with awkard hardiness, "Oh, come on now! That's my girl! This'll do!"

Only to hear her insist, "But don't be *ridic*, Daddy. It won't at all! Take it back."

And for a moment he stood staring at her, before he felt her take his hand and put the polish back in it.

It was such a small thing, such a little thing—and yet Charlie had often caught himself remembering it.

Once, when Charlie was in college and Gussie was preparing for Princeton, his father had written him:

"Thank God Gus is not one of these namby-pamby English majors, but entering business school, ready to enter industry, a man's world! You'll probably be an English teacher!" and Charlie reacted to the letter with contempt for his father, wrote him that he didn't care to emulate him—or anyone like him—cheap money-makers of the world.

Was there the same gap between Janie and himself? Had it always been there without his knowing it? Always since the day he felt her put the bottle of polish back in his hand? Was that the beginning?

". . . Marriage is out!"

Charlie thought of Marge Mann's kneeling nude before him.

"My God, Janie!" he said aloud. "Don't screw yourself up like this! How can I tell you not to?"

"You see, Dad, Dud is a writer . . . you deal with hacks who sell ideas down the river for three cents a word."

Otto Avery . . . Charlie could see in his mind Avery's image on a television screen, then a blackout, and he remembered—very vaguely—a poem he had written in college, something about breakfast with Mitzie Thompson, and he remembered how she had told him she knew he'd be a writer, a famous one, an important one, and how he'd believed it. God, it was funny— Life was so different than you'd thought it would be.

Charlie gulped his drink, got up and got another.

". . . life has to be meaningful to me, to Dud, to people like us, life has to have a message, something more than the business world step-on-toes-and-go-for-the-buck."

Whose toes had *he* ever stepped on reaching for the buck?

He heard Avery's voice? "This is the news and my views on the news."

And he thought, "Goddam pansy!"

But he felt no satisfaction thinking that. And he was getting a little high. He thought that if he had married

Mitzie Thompson, married someone like her, who had
believed so in him, he would have been that writer,
and that he ought to crash in the goddam door of the
guest room and make Joan fix him something to eat;
the least she could do. His gut was empty. He hadn't
eaten since lunch, and it occurred to him it was a
corny thing for Joan to do, give him the shoes for his
birthday. But she was kind of a corny woman; wouldn't
catch her swallowing pills in the toilet (age sixty, naked
and begging for a drink; a C-cup bitch, all right—Wally
Keene was right).

"Ever hear of a C-cup bitch before, Charlie?"

He saw Keene's ugly face, remembered Marge crying, "I need love," and thought vaguely of an inn in
Vermont, coming from the cold window which he had
rushed across the room to open, back into her arms;
and the warmth, and the way he thought he loved her
then.

". . . suburbia wear comfortable shoes; read Doctor
Spock; play Scrabble after dinner monotony——"

Charlie folded the letter and put it in his pocket, got
up, drank his whisky and went for more.

Again he saw the shoes.

He tried to remember what he had been like when
Joan and he lived on Bleecker Street. It was funny
the little things he could remember, the dank smell of
cats in the halls, and the darkness of those halls, coming out from them into the sunlight of a warm day . . .
and at night, tripping over the fat Italian mammas who
sat fanning themselves on the stoops, shopping in the
open market with Joan, the naive excitement of finding
fruits and vegetables neither knew about, buying flowers from some old woman on a street corner, the glow
they had from the small and the trivial, the everyday
game of their routine. What had he been like? Ingen-
uous? Eager? Young? Sure?

Yes. And had he changed so much?

He was proud now, too proud to go up and tell

Bruce that the *Vile* dummy is every bit that vile . . .
And why proud?

It was odd that he thought: Because of Gussie;
caught himself in the slip; meant to think Wally Keene;
would never have taken a back seat to Keene or anyone like Keene when he was younger. But now?

He thought grimly, Keene is right about Marge;
she had to go. Marge's pride wrecked her too. Always
too proud to admit the truth. Pull herself up by her
own bootstraps. She always said she could.

"Charlie," she used to say, "I don't have to answer
to anyone, and the reason for that is I've never had
to ask anyone for anything. I go on my own power.
I have plenty of power!"

Charlie got up and began to pace the room, mumbling to himself, feeling the bourbon inside of him now,
faintly conscious of the fact he had told Joan not to
buy the good bourbon for Manhattans . . . remembering that she had had people for dinner for his birthday and the good bourbon would be in the kitchen up
on the shelf above the sink. But that was no excuse to
lock him out when he was fifty years old. But as he
thought this he talked about Marge, muttering to himself:

"No, she didn't want to depend on anyone, but she
had to get plastered to show her feelings. She couldn't
ever say anything right out. Just like my mother used
to be—exactly that way. Somehow they make *you* feel
rotten. Waiting in that hospital corridor tonight to be
sure she was all right—made me pay for firing her. Had
that operation and didn't tell anyone, but drank so
goddam much in the end people had to take care of
her. Proud bitch! Too proud! Aw, God, Marge messed
herself up badly. A mess. Mess."

Charlie stopped before the eagle mirror hung above
the couch.

His reflection frowned at him.

"A mess," he said. "A mess . . . Fifty years old and
the wife in the guest room with the door locked. No

footstool and my daughter sleeping around from here to hell and gone. And every color of the rainbow in my living room . . . A mess!"

Then he fell onto the couch and slept.

MARCH 7, 1957

CHAPTER TWENTY-TWO

AT FOUR in the morning the couple sat in the living room of the Davises' home in Boston.

They were alone, watching the white coals of a fire burn out. It was snowing outside. Dudley could remember that the only words he could think to say to his parents when he brought Jayne into this room hours earlier this evening, were, "Snowing out. Really coming down," and as he said them, he felt suddenly young and ineffectual and naive. Her fingers had tightened on his arm, and he had thought of the young man in the play *Our Town,* when on his wedding day he stood facing his bride, oddly frightened and unwilling to have happen to him that which was happening.

Dudley's father said, "That *is* a surprise."

Goddam right it is, Dudley thought, and he heard Jayne's voice crack as she answered, "Yes, it is, isn't it," and the slight edge of suspicion to his mother's, "Yes, it is."

Then, unable to live out the niceties, or suffer through the small talk, unwilling to explain, yet unable to avoid the explanation, in an awkward and naked compulsive manner, before he had even unbuttoned his topcoat or taken Jayne's mouton from her shoulders, he stood and almost hollered, "Jayne and I have to be married immediately!"

His father had looked at both of them blankly for a moment.

His mother had said, startled, "Oh?"

Until, "Take your coats off and sit down," his father had managed finally.

And Dudley, with whatever illogical relentlessness was driving him to make the announcement angrily, had added, "she's three months' gone."

Jayne, of course, had burst into tears instantly.

Mrs. Davis followed the same course.

The ice was broken.

Now that it was over, he had his arm around her, thinking as he studied her profile that this was going to be it; *this* was; and that. It was all right.

"Not tired, are you?" he said.

"I couldn't sleep."

"Neither could I," he said. "I'm glad we came. You are too, aren't you?"

"At first I was scared. But they made it easy for us, Dud. They were so nice about it."

"I knew they'd come through. Tradition and all. After all, it's a Davis; not the first one weaned on a gun either."

"Don't talk that way."

"We might as well face it," he said. "Do you know something?"

"What?"

"I'm glad it happened. I'm actually glad. I never would have had the sense to know I wanted to marry you. You'd have married someone else probably."

"We're not going to change, are we, Dud? I mean we're not going to be like everyone else when the baby comes?"

"We'll put him in a knapsack and take him everywhere we go," he said.

"I wish it were morning."

"It is."

"No, I mean, I wish it were late enough to call Dad."

"Soon enough," he said, "but do you really think you

should tell him over the phone? Can't you wait until
we go into the city for the license?"

She said, "No, I'm going to call him."

"What do you think he'll say?"

"I just don't know," she said. "I just don't know."

MARCH 7, 1957

CHAPTER TWENTY-THREE

CHARLIE GIBSON woke after an hour. It was still dark
out, and the lights blazed in the room around him.
Beside the leg of the couch, the half-empty glass of
bourbon rested, and the letter from Janie had fallen
from his pocket onto the floor.

He looked at his watch and saw that it was fifteen
minutes past four. He still felt a little foggy, high.
Getting up, Charlie went to the front door through
the hallway, opened it and breathed in the cold March
air. He looked across the street at the Marksons', wondering why he felt some preposterous satisfaction in
the knowledge that all seemed serene there. And then,
he glanced next door at the Lederers'. He remembered
a couple of months back when Ashley Lederer lost his
job; just got dumped—wham-o, like that!—out of a
$30,000 a year P.R. job. He remembered how Mil,
Ashley's wife, tried to cover for him, saying Ash had
always wanted to free-lance and Ash himself coming
right out with it one night at the club—sober, too; saying, "I was fired. And I'm plenty worried about getting
something else. Man my age, for the love of Pete!"
Charlie remembered that Bruce interviewed Ashley
almost the next day, after Markson got him an interview at a colleague's firm; and Charlie remembered
when Ashley finally got placed—for more than he'd

been making in P.R. Well, Charlie felt great, he remembered. God damn it, when Ash got that break Charlie felt great. And the only time he'd probably ever see Ash before spring, when they'd wave casually from their lawns, would be if Ash wanted to borrow a snow shovel, or if Charlie'd forgotten his chains and wanted a push.

It was funny all right, Charlie thought. God damn it, it was nice. He decided he was either drunk or a candidate for the laughing academy to be standing on his front porch at four in the morning waxing sentimental over a bastard like Ashley Lederer who couldn't even keep his hedges clipped. Or Mel Markson, a lousy cheapskate who still drove a '41 Buick. Likes their lines, the '41's, he claims, goddam rubbish, Charlie thought; cheapskate. Charlie grinned. Yep, he was off his rocker, all right, standing out at the crack of dawn choking up over his neighbors.

He took a deep breath, one last one, went in and shut the door behind him. Again he tripped on the edge of the coat rack. Some day he'd kill himself that way.

Charlie walked into the living room and reached down to take the letter from Janie from the rug. He decided to answer it before he went to bed. He decided he could do that much anyway. With it, Charlie went to his den, around the corner from the kitchen near the rear staircase, and sitting down at his desk there, shooting a clean piece of paper into the roller, Charlie began to type.

CHAPTER TWENTY-FOUR

DEAR JANIE (Jaynie)

Your father is a little high; he thinks, with good reason.

In this world of comfortable shoes, Dr. Spock and Scrabble after dinner, he finds himself in the awkward position of being locked out of the bedroom by your mother. And yesterday he was fifty years old. He received your letter about Dudley Davis, and he suddenly realized he had no answer for you, only some stray and sundry thoughts to pass along to you.

This then, in the form of an answer.

You're right to say I never failed you—along material lines. I wanted you to have everything, and I think I provided you with everything you wanted—in the way of schools, clothes, allowance and so forth. You were more or less handed these things on a silver platter.

But honey, I think I failed you by never telling you that the platter wasn't just pulled out of the butler's pantry, but that it was worked for.

When you were born—and what a squalling brat you were—and what a terror that first year—your mother and I sat up nights thinking of ways to slash the budget to afford you, and through the years we planned and saved so that you could enjoy the things we've given you and hope to give you in the future.

I don't tell you this to say, "See what we've done for you, see how we've sacrificed," but to explain to you that you are the end product of the two machineries which, in your letter, you most abhorred, the business world and marriage. And the struggle within both for success.

You're right in believing the business world is not all lollipops and luncheon dates, but neither is it all "step-on-the-toes-and-go-for-the-buck." Like any other world, what it is depends on what you are. Like any .other world, it has its stereotypes and clichés, its ruts and necessities, and its challenges, casualties, triumphs and tragedies.

Your young man wants to be a writer, a serious writer, and that's a fine ambition. But in the writers' world too there are the ruthless and the kind, the monotonous and the vital. No one world holds a monopoly on either good or bad, more "meaningful" or more "meaningless."

As a lad, I believed I'd be a poet or a novelist, a renowned one. I imagined I'd have several alluring and fawning mistresses, and maybe a wife, and at the chance of shocking *you*, I never, not even when your mother told me you were on the way, wanted children to have any part in my life.

Now at 50 I find myself an editor in a chain magazine house, who rarely even gets the opportunity to read poems or novels; on the verge, after this letter is written, of trying to persuade the woman I have been married to for 22 years to unlock the door of the guest bedroom and come on into ours (because your father never rests comfortably unless he sees the curler-pinned head on the pillow of the bed opposite him) and attempting in a clumsily affectionate way to tell the other woman he loves—you—how many good things he wants for her, not material things, but cliché things he never thought he'd endorse as a boy. Marriage, and a family, and some certain place in the community of people.

This isn't quite the world I imagined and dreamed of in my younger days, but it's very nice all the same—and that's the way in this life. One's prayers and wishes are usually granted, but often the fullfillment is quite different—and much better—than the wish.

I can't advise you, sweetheart, but I can hope for you, that somehow this feeling you have which is "more than love" will bring what love brings—the immense complexity involved in being not different from everyone else, and not exactly like everyone else, but more or less the way people are in all worlds: unwilling, protesting, happy, sort of soaring along without knowing it.

This, in place of an answer.

                                                  Love,
                                                  DAD

MARCH 7, 1957

CHAPTER TWENTY-FIVE

IT WAS six forty-five in the morning when Charlie finished what he had begun after he had written Janie.

Carefully, he began to reread the memo he had worked over:

RE: THE VILE DUMMY

One of the principle reasons this book is a mistake is that it will alienate a major advertising account—the sponsors of Avery's shows, who take full-page advertsements in seven of our books, including the weekly, *Topic*.

They have built the name Avery, and vice versa, and to attack him is to attack them, so closely associated are they in the mind of the consumer.

In addition, it is obvious that—

Suddenly, Charlie put the pencil down and let the memo fall to the desk. He began to wonder just what in hell he was doing writing a memo to Bruce. Why didn't he just *tell* Bruce? Why hadn't he told him before this? . . . He was immensely ashamed to believe that Wally Keene could have even in any small way been the reason, so ashamed that he guffawed aloud. My God, Charlie, whata you know about that.

Impulsively he wadded up the memo. He would remember it, all right! And before he got up to Bruce's office, he'd get the sales figures on the last issue of the Dorset book which ran the banner on the cover with the Hemingway piece.

That was what Cadence needed more than they needed a new book; they needed to do something about the old ones. They needed banners and big-name writers, and they needed to promote hell out of them —billboards, radio spots across the board canned for national consumption. They needed to spark up what they had. What the hell made Bruce sell Cadence down the river for a book on queers and creeps and crackpots? Charlie was going to ask him just what the hell Bruce was thinking of. Never mind if it's in dummy. Never mind if it's in mock-up. Shove it! Can it!

The hell with a memo!

Charlie leaned back in his desk chair and laughed.

Then, stretching, he pulled himself to his feet. He felt good, better than he'd felt in a long time. He wanted to go up and pound on Joan's door and tell her how he felt, and as he stood there staring out at the beginning blue of early morning, he began to resent her locking him out without even waiting to hear his side. And as suddenly as he had felt the resentment, he felt a certain resignation, and a flash of uncanny loneliness.

He thought of how really alone people could be— not for long, not most people, but for those suspended moments of utter isolation. And he thought of Marge waking up in a bed in the hospital, and he stood staring at the day with an empty feeling, wishing Joan would appear miraculously, like the wife in some slick story, with a pot of hot coffee on a tray, and a smile and a kiss.

But God, he was too tired now. He decided to go up to bed and sleep the few hours left before it would be time once more to catch the New York bound.

After he put out the light, Charlie went up the stairs, past "Janie & Mamma, Glen Falls, 1936—Picnic" and "Papa's new car & Janie, 1946" and on down the hall toward the bedroom.

In her bed across from him, Joan was asleep.

Quietly Charlie slipped out of his clothes and under the covers in his own bed.

At some point in the night, she had come back to their room. She had met him halfway. The rest was up to him when they woke up, and Charlie grinned as he shut his eyes.

That's right, he thought, it never works out quite the way you dreamed it would in this life. But somehow it does work out.

It isn't total one-hundred percent-Ivory-Soap perfect. Nothing is.

But it's okay.

Charlie Gibson was just dropping off to sleep then, when the telephone began its persistent ringing.